BEYOND
*E*ARTH'S
HORIZON

By ANTHONY FUCILLA

Published 2021 by arima publishing

www.arimapublishing.com

ISBN 978 1 84549 784 2

© Anthony Fucilla 2021

Swirl is an imprint of arima publishing.

arima publishing
ASK House, Northgate Avenue
Bury St Edmunds, Suffolk IP32 6BB
t: (+44) 01284 700321

www.arimapublishing.com

BEYOND EARTH'S HORIZON

BY ANTHONY FUCILLA

This book is dedicated to my dear friend Ronald 'Bud' Pope...

Cover Design: Gary Pope

Mathematics is a powerful guide to the realms of reality... It leads us directly to the possibility that there are more than three dimensions of space...

Foreword

In Beyond Earth's Horizon, Anthony once again presents his readers with a fascinating array of factual information regarding our Universe and predictions of what the future may hold. But in this adventure he takes us one step further and explores what might lie beyond our own reality. As well as current thinking concerning the existence and formation of parallel universes, he reflects on how societies within those universes might differ from our own and how the historical development and constraints of society affect scientific discovery and technological advancement.

Alternate universes, a surveillance state, mind control, enslaved preserved brains, existence beyond death and the fomentation of rebellion are all the facets which, interwoven with scientific theory, make this a unique and thought-provoking read.

Editor: Vicky C. Sheppard

BEYOND EARTH'S HORIZON

R1 cruised smoothly above the city of Philadelphia at a speed that was within the legal limit, running almost silently on its unrestricted fuel supply culled from interstellar hydrogen. Scattered below, dots of colourful light flickered to and fro in the evening darkness, and to Gregory, it seemed as if they formed a bizarre yet somehow transcendental pattern.

Then the wind picked up, shaking him from his reverie. Lightning cracked where scattered cloud boiled in the night sky. Earth shivered as the atmospheric discharges rolled... Orienting himself, he focused on the sea of switches and dials that lay before him. He noticed that one, the temperature regulator, was glowing a dull red indicating that it was out of operation. An electrical fault, he thought. His expert fingers danced over the controls. He reached over and began to fiddle with the faulty dial. The dull red glow suddenly turned bright green. Problem solved! He turned it and cool air began to circle about him. He then lay back and gazed out at the full Moon. It hung bright and majestic as a thin nocturnal cloud crossed its face.

Earthlight always illuminated the near-side of the Moon, something that the far-side never experienced as a result of tidal locking. He felt a warm glow as the sight triggered memories of the comfortable underground lunar resort he had visited many years back. Experiencing low-gravity movements there was dream-like... he thought. He recalled the moment when he went through the ship's air lock and the tube joining it to the station entrance. He then began to think about the infinity between Earth and the Moon. Their closeness, their gravitational interplay, the tidal stresses; At eighty times the mass of the Moon, the Earth caused significant unbalanced stresses on its satellite which in turn caused weak lunar quakes. A Moonquake could last for an hour due to the lack of water to dampen the seismic vibrations. Gregory was grateful he had never experienced one during his brief visit.

Suddenly a voice blared from the speaker above his head. It was the AI system, R1. "Professor Seymour we shall be descending shortly Sir. We are approaching your final destination for this evening, home..."

"That's great R1," he replied as if communicating with a human being, a functioning nervous system with an engrammatic pattern of experience. It was not that dissimilar, he mused. In this case it was a nonhuman nervous system but R1 operated, spoke, reacted and navigated as if it were alive, as if it had synapse function, a continuous field of thought and reaction. The complexity of the system, the machine, was in a sense responsible for the development of a form of robotic consciousness that literally gave the impression that one was speaking to a living system; an entity in its own right, with a strong mechanical personality that was able to indulge in the most complex of discussions. Yet R1 was still just a humble hover-car and now began a prompt yet controlled descent. The trajectory was marked out on a luminous screen. Out in the distance, a police-vehicle glided by, framed by the night sky. Its signal lights flashed red and blue. He gazed over at it absently thinking that he'd soon be home...

Inside the comfort of his home, he walked into the high-ceilinged living room. "Lights," he declared and with the sharp command of his voice, soft lights instantly activated. He walked to the small bar which was nestled artistically in one corner. He took a glass, then a bottle of whiskey and poured handsomely. Once that task was complete, he made his way to the large white sofa and sank contentedly into its soft plushness. He began to drink and relax, thinking back over his day. It had not been a particularly hard one, but weariness dragged at his mind. As a lecturing university Professor, it had presented nothing other than the usual chores. He pulled a large cigar from his jacket pocket, struck it to life, took a long pull and watched the smoke rising and fading. His eyes now merrily sought the large picture that was pinned to the cream wall. A picture of Planet Earth framed in space... He noted the all too familiar luminous astronomical details printed below the image and raised his glass taking a sip of whiskey:

Mean Orbital velocity: 66000 miles per hour

Orbital eccentricity: 0.017

Mean surface gravitational acceleration of the rotating earth: 32.174 feet per second per second

The sudden patter of naked feet shattered his concentration... His wife Elaine walked in surrounded by an aura of shining loveliness, gracious as ever. Tonight, she was dressed in a pink flowing gown which clung seductively to her voluptuous figure. Her green eyes sparkled and her neatly fixed head of hair was as black as ebony.

"Elaine, you're still up?" he asked rhetorically. He puffed hard on his cigar; its tip waxed and waned. Then a faint smile played over his lips.

She padded over and sat beside him, her beauty flashing like a meteor.

"I couldn't sleep..." Her soft, elegant French-Canadian accent made him tingle and as their eyes connected, their warm lips met in a shared kiss.

Gently, they pulled away but their gaze remained locked. He suddenly noticed that the pleasure and love her eyes had initially radiated was becoming overshadowed by a sad pleading. That question again! Sighing softly, he placed the cigar into the nearby tray, took another sip of whiskey, put the glass down and said, "I guess you've still got your mind set on Montreal?" He looked sour now.

"Gregory," it's my home city, all my family are there." She spoke in a low, hurried tone, toying with the gold ring on her finger.

He shrugged as if resigned to the fact that one day he'd have to give in.

"Besides," she exclaimed, "Canada is such a beautiful country... all that fresh air, beautiful forests, lakes, rivers and mountains."

"Yes sweetheart, but as I have explained, my job here at the university is so important to me. I've spent years with the faculty; I'm highly respected within my field."

"Yes Gregory, you are. You could easily get a transfer to another university. Montreal has many. You would easily get a post. Not to mention that with your inheritance you don't really need to work anyway."

"Elaine," he paused and could not help a warm smile as he continued, "I was born to lecture, born to impart my knowledge within the scholastic system. It's what I do best. I'm compelled regardless of our economic status. I love what I do. I need to continue at least for a little while longer, then we will see."

"Okay, I understand that, but why not in Montreal, in Canada...? Besides, Philadelphia has become way too overpopulated. At least think about it seriously."

He could not find the right words so he placed his hands on her shoulders and just nodded in partial agreement. Then in the silence of the night he wrapped her in an embrace so she could not see his face.

In the bleak grey of early morning Gregory was sitting in his office at the university, his feet turned outwards, his brown hair smoothed down either side of his parting. Although in work-mode, he was unusually tired, lack of sleep the cause. He closed his eyes and rubbed his forehead with a heavy hand. The tiny wall clock ticked away. On his desk was an old book which his father had given him during his teens, a sentimental thing. It was entitled: Great Scientists from the past. It was open at Planck's quantum theory – light and energy come in little packets not continuous streams. A sudden knock made him jump. It could be the Dean of the university, he thought and the sleepy feeling at once drained away at that realisation.

"Err, yes," he said and the metallic door swung open. He relaxed again when he saw it was his friend, Sheldon van den Berg.

"Gregory, do you have a minute...?"

"Sheldon... Of course, take a seat my friend."

Sheldon walked in slowly and sat; a tall, thin man, with blond hair running to silver and clean shaven. There was something in his eyes that silenced Gregory for a time.

"Is everything okay...?" he asked, eventually.

Sheldon hesitated for a fraction of a second... "Gregory, this is a slightly unusual request."

"What is it you are requesting?"

"That you indulge me for a while. Gregory we are both top professors here at the university...You in astronomy and me, psychology. Two top minds in our respective fields."

"Yes, that goes without saying, and...?"

Sheldon licked his moist lips and replied, "What if I told you that last night, I experienced something that falls into the category of the unexplained... the paranormal, almost supernatural?"

Gregory leaned back in his chair and folded his arms. His eyes widened and his forehead creased.

19

"Sheldon, we've known each other a very long time. You're a friend. You're a top mind. My respect for you is immense. Now, tell me, what did you see?"

Sheldon still hesitated. He stood up, paced the floor, then returned and leant against the desk, his eyes a wall of concentration.

"Okay Gregory... These are the sequence of events as they happened. Please indulge me..." Sheldon paused again and gazed at the floor. He then looked up and said, "Last night on my route home, I witnessed something that was simply extraordinary. We had reached cruising altitude, when a large, blue sphere of light suddenly shimmered into existence in the sky ahead diagonally to my left. It was a brilliant blue contrasting strongly against the dark of night."

Seconds of silence passed as their eyes locked...

"It was overwhelming, it was like time ceased. Next my hover-car was pulled towards this blue light as if it were controlled by an unseen force. The AI

20

system fought to regain control, but it failed. I was in a complete state of fear and panic and knowing that it was simply my subconscious mind emitting the glandular-vascular-cardiac-visceral impulses associated with fear did not make it any better."

Sheldon paused, his cheeks slightly red. His eyes widened as he recaptured a particular moment.

"Then, just as I was about to pass through what I can only describe as an opening, an opening in space, almost like a doorway, the light suddenly vanished. The AI system regained full control..."

"Remarkable," muttered Gregory softly. He licked his lips and groomed his left ear with his hand, scratching sharply. "That's indeed remarkable... I do not, cannot doubt the legitimacy of your story given that I know you so well Sheldon and that you can be sure of with all certainty."

Sheldon dropped back into the chair, crossing his legs and asked, "In your opinion Gregory what was it?"

"It's impossible to say or give a definitive answer. Our universe is so complex and mysterious. We pretend to know much, but really we know nothing. Humanity is still in the dark."

"Indeed. You know Gregory... the more we seek to learn and understand the more we realise we ultimately know nothing."

"Correct my friend. Remember Sheldon, space itself is far more complex than we could ever think... the fundamental structure of space, its intrinsic energies, and so on... the quantum fluctuations that embodied the energies of space itself. Remember empty space is not empty at all. Nothing is more crowded than empty space. Every point in space contains information. It's a bubbling brew of virtual particles constantly popping in and out of existence. This in turn means that there's an invisible field everywhere in the universe. In essence we live in a giant cosmic superconductor. This opening that you speak of was perhaps a doorway into another dimension."

"Another dimension...? You mean a parallel dimension, an alternate reality...?"

"Yes, parallel universes are self-contained planes of existence, co-existing with our own. It's quite a fascinating subject. Just think, is there another 'You' out there in a parallel universe? I think this subject is one of the most exciting and mysterious topics within the realms of physics... Perhaps there are other universes perhaps even with different versions of us, different histories and alternate outcomes than our own. Perhaps there is a universe out there where everything happens exactly as in this one. Perhaps there is a universe out there for every outcome that's imaginable. If the universes are all the same as one another in terms of physical laws, and if the number of these universes are truly infinite, and if the many-world interpretation of quantum mechanics is totally valid, does that imply that there are parallel universes out there where everything in them evolved precisely the same as our own universe did, except with one tiny quantum outcome which was different?"

"Gregory, this is fascinating, but does it have anything to do with observable, measurable reality? From a purely physics point of view, I'm sure parallel universes are a fascinating idea, but surely it is very difficult to test. If I understand it correctly, quantum physics is notorious for having unpredictable outcomes. If you take a single electron and shoot it through a double slit, you can only know the probabilities of where it will land. You cannot predict exactly where it will show up..."

"Well Sheldon, one remarkable idea, known as the many-worlds interpretation of quantum mechanics, postulates that all the outcomes that can possibly occur actually do occur, but only one outcome can happen in each Universe. It takes an infinite number of parallel Universes to account for all the possibilities. There are no experiments or observations that rule it out. Another place where parallel Universes arise in physics is from the whole notion of the multiverse..."

From a small black remote, Gregory activated a switch and the wall-screen behind them came into life with a hum. He pointed and Sheldon turned.

Pictures and diagrams formed and flashed across the screen. It was a visual explanation of how the multiverse operated in terms of physics. Gregory continued...

"Our highly complex, convoluted Universe began approximately 13.8 billion years ago with the Big Bang... All matter in the Universe was condensed to a point. Then a mind-shattering, fine-tuned explosion took place... Furthermore the Universe was not constant in space or in time, but rather has evolved from a more uniform, hotter, denser state to a clumpier, cooler and more diffuse state today. As a result, this has given us an interestingly rich and glorious Universe, a Universe peppered with many generations of stars. In addition, our Universe as far as powerful telescopes can see, is vast and immense. Including photons, which are the fundamental particle of light, and neutrinos, our Universe contains some 10^{90} particles, clumped and clustered together into hundreds of billions to trillions of galaxies. Each galaxy contains around a trillion stars and they are scattered across the cosmos in a sphere some 93 billion light years in diameter, at least from our perspective...

Now Sheldon, the reason the Universe appears finite in size, the reason we can't see anything that's more than a specific distance away isn't because the Universe is actually finite in terms of its size but is rather because the Universe has only existed in its present state for a finite amount of time. That limit is set by the distance that light has had to travel since the instant of the Big Bang... Having said this, this in no way implies that there aren't more Universes out there beyond the segment that's accessible to us. In fact, we have every reason to believe with immense certainty that there is a lot more, infinitely more, from both theoretical and observational points of view. In addition, what we find is the Universe is most consistent with being spatially flat, with being uniform over a volume that is much greater than the volume of the piece of the Universe that is observable to us, thus most likely containing more universe that's incredibly similar to our own for hundreds of billions of light years in all directions beyond what the eye can see."

He coughed... his throat raw from talking... but this was his passion. Wiping his forehead, he continued...

"Now, back to the Big Bang... The Big Bang itself wasn't the very beginning. There was a very different phase of the Universe that occurred previously to set up and give rise to this incredible event, and that was cosmological inflation. That phase, a period of cosmological inflation, describes a phase where rather than being full of radiation and matter, the Universe was filled with energy inherent to space itself... a state that causes the Universe to expand at an exponential rate. Now, obviously the Universe didn't continue to expand forever, because we're here, thus inflation had to come to an end, setting up this mind-blowing event that took place approximately 13.8 billion years ago that we call, the Big Bang. Also, we are not sure how long this inflationary state lasted. Furthermore, inflation is rather like a wave that spreads out over time, a bit like a quantum field. This means, as time goes on and more and more space gets created due to inflation, particular regions, probabilistically, are going to be more likely to see inflation come to an end, while other regions will be more likely to see inflation continue. Regions where inflation ends will give rise to a Big Bang and a universe similar to ours, while the regions where it doesn't will continue to inflate for a longer period. As time goes on because of the dynamics of expansion, no two regions where inflation ends will ever interact or collide. The regions where inflation doesn't end will expand between them, literally pushing them apart. Thus when and where inflation ends, a Big Bang takes place. But inflation doesn't end everywhere at once. Places where inflation doesn't end continue to inflate, this of course, is logical... This in turn gives rise to more space... and of course, more potential Big Bangs. Once inflation starts, it's almost impossible to stop it from occurring. As time elapses, more Big Bangs, all detached from one another, take place giving rise to a large number of independent universes... This is known as the multiverse. Not only would these other universes be out there, but matter and energy from them would have the capability of crossing over to and interacting with matter and energy in our own Universe...."

Sheldon checked his wristwatch and stood... his expression somewhat enigmatic.

"Gregory, I'm so sorry, I've got to leave you now. Fascinating discussion but I can't be late for class. Can we continue this later?"

"Sure Sheldon...!" exclaimed Gregory.

"I feel this is something that needs to be discussed further." Sheldon paused, then shook his head as if to clear it. "I keep picturing the moment that blue light appeared. Had I told anyone else, they would have found it hard to believe..."

Sheldon smiled... a dull, almost forced smile. He drifted toward the door, and walked out, closing it behind him. There was a pause and Gregory imagined his friend taking a few deep breaths. Seconds later he could hear Sheldon walking away his steps slowly fading into silence. Gregory sat back in his chair contemplating the discussion and

Sheldon's strange encounter... He rubbed his jaw in thought, almost transfixed by the whole notion of alternate realities, parallel universes, and his eyes grew wide at the sheer complexity and elegance of it all. A vision of what an alternate reality could really be like played across his mind.

But reality had to intrude at some point and the afternoon found him standing in a brightly lit lecture hall with a group of students ranged before him. He was going through some fairly basic stuff for university level students, but high schools were variable, and he found it useful to get everyone on the same basic page before they got into the more complex stuff.

"Saturn, a gas giant with an average radius of about nine times that of Earth is the sixth planet from the Sun and the second-largest in the Solar-System; the largest planet being Jupiter... Saturn is called a gas giant because it is predominantly composed of hydrogen and helium. Furthermore, it lacks a definite surface, though it may have a solid core.

Saturn's interior is most likely composed of a core of iron-nickel and rock. This core is surrounded by a deep layer of metallic hydrogen, an intermediate layer of liquid hydrogen and liquid helium, and finally a gaseous outer layer."

He paused and rubbed his jaw, casting his eyes over his young audience. He was pleased to see they were mostly still eager and alert. He crossed to his desk and sat for the next part of his presentation.

"Furthermore, the gas giant Saturn has a pale-yellow hue due to the ammonia crystals in its upper atmosphere," he continued. "An electrical current within the metallic hydrogen layer is thought to give rise to Saturn's planetary magnetic field. And so, we come to its moons; at least 82 moons are known to orbit Saturn, Titan being the largest and incidentally it has the honour of being the second largest in the Solar System. The outer atmosphere of Saturn contains 96.3% molecular hydrogen and 3.25% helium by volume. Trace amounts of ammonia, acetylene, ethane, methane, propane and phosphine have been detected in Saturn's atmosphere. The upper clouds are composed of ammonia crystals."

"Professor Seymour," suddenly exploded a female student, interrupting his flow. "I've heard that you are planning to take us all on a space-cruise as part of the syllabus. Is this true?"

He suppressed a grin. Kirsten was an odd combination of extremely shy and extremely enthusiastic. She had obviously been bottling this question up. It was off topic, but he decided to indulge her.

"Yes, it is, Kirsten. There's nothing better than experiencing a brief journey into outer-space. For a student of astronomy it is the ultimate experience and would benefit you all greatly. However, for us to get the okay, there's a long process and various channels to go through before a decision is made. I've spoken to the Dean and he thinks it's a great idea. Let's see..."

He halted, and refocused....

"Now, back to our gas giant... Saturn's most famous feature is its prominent ring system, which is composed mostly of ice particles, with a smaller amount of rocky debris and dust. This makes it visually unique. The rings extend from 6,630 to 120,700 kilometres outward from Saturn's equator and average approximately 20 meters in thickness. Incidentally, the other gas giants also have ring systems, however Saturn's is the most visible and the largest. With regard to the origin of the rings, there are two possibilities: One hypothesis suggests that the rings are remnants of a destroyed moon of Saturn, and the second hypothesis proposes that the rings are left over from the original nebular material from which Saturn was formed..."

There was a brief pause.

"Now we move on to the planet Neptune... Cold, dark and whipped by supersonic winds, the ice giant Neptune is a fascinating planet. In fact Neptune is the solar system's windiest planet. Clouds of frozen methane scud across the surface at speeds of more than 2,000 km/h. More than thirty times as far from the sun as Earth, Neptune is the only planet in the solar system not visible to the naked eye. Like Jupiter and Saturn, Neptune's atmosphere is composed primarily of hydrogen and helium, along with traces of hydrocarbons and possibly nitrogen... Neptune's internal structure resembles that of Uranus. Its atmosphere forms about 5% to 10% of its mass and extends perhaps 10% to 20% of the way towards the core, where it reaches pressures of about 10 GPa... The average distance between Neptune and the Sun is 4.5 billion km, and it completes an orbit on average every 164.79 years... The planet's orbit has a profound impact on the region directly beyond it. This is known as the Kuiper belt which is a ring of small icy worlds very similar to an asteroid belt but far bigger. Neptune has fourteen known moons."

Again, a brief pause...

"Switching planets again, Uranus is known as the sideways planet because it rotates on its side. It has twenty-seven known moons. Like Neptune and Jupiter, Uranus is a ringed planet. Its unique sideways rotation makes for weird seasons and the planet's north pole experiences 21 years of night-time in winter, 21 years of daytime in summer and 42 years of day and night in the spring and fall. Uranus orbits the Sun once every 84 years. The rotational period of the interior of Uranus is 17 hours, 14 minutes. As with all the giant planets, its upper atmosphere experiences strong winds in the direction of its rotation. Furthermore, at some latitudes, such as about sixty degrees south, visible features of the atmosphere move much faster, making a full rotation in as little as 14 hours...."

"Professor Seymour," another enthusiastic voice, this time male, took advantage of his pause for breath. "I know that this does not tie in with today's lecture, but I really wanted to ask you this question."

Maybe he did not have them quite as captivated as he had thought but they were at least keen and showing interest in the subject.

"Sure, go ahead," he encouraged.

"With regard to physical cosmology... how will the universe end, in your opinion?"

"Well Jones, known science suggests there are three possible theories and I will touch on all three very briefly. The first is known as the Big Crunch... the Closed Universe. In short, the density of the universe is more than five atoms of hydrogen per cubic metre. Thus there's no repulsive effect of dark energy, and gravity eventually halts the universe's expansion. With contraction, all the matter in the universe collapses to a point. In summary the Big Crunch is a hypothetical scenario for the ultimate fate of the Universe, in which the expansion of the Universe eventually reverses and it re-collapses, ultimately causing the cosmic scale factor to reach zero, an event potentially followed by a reformation of the Universe starting with another Big Bang... The other way is known as the Big Rip... the Open Universe. Now, if space is curved and open, the Universe, in principle, will continue to expand forever and dark energy will help drive this continual expansion. As a result there is heat death. The Big Rip or otherwise known as the Big Freeze then takes place. Again, in summary, the Big Rip is basically a hypothetical cosmological model concerning the final fate of the universe, in which the matter of the universe, from stars and galaxies to atoms and subatomic particles, and even space-time itself, is progressively torn apart by the expansion at a certain time in the future, until the distances between particles become infinite... Finally, there's the Flat Universe theory... With no dark energy a flat universe will expand forever at a decelerating rate. With dark energy the expansion initially slows, and this is because of gravity. It then speeds up. As a result, the Universe's fate is basically the same as the Open Universe theory bringing us back to The Big Rip or The Big Freeze."

"Professor," said Jones. "One more thing... Am I correct in saying that approximately sixty-eight per cent of the Universe is made up of dark energy?"

"Yes indeed, and it is the driving force that causes the galaxies to move apart in an almost eternal continual expansion. The truth is nobody really knows what dark energy actually is. In fact, we don't even know how strong it is. More is unknown than is known."

Seconds of silence fell...

"We do know how much dark energy there is because we know how it affects the Universe's expansion. Other than that, it is a complete mystery. But it is an important mystery. As you correctly stated, approximately sixty-eight per cent of the universe is dark energy. Dark matter makes up about twenty-seven per cent. The rest, everything on Earth, everything ever observed with all of our instruments, all normal matter, adds up to less than five per cent of the Universe. Anyway the best way to explain dark energy is that it acts like anti-gravity. It pushes the Universe apart. As the gravity of dark matter tries to pull the Universe together, in turn dark energy tries to push it apart. Around five billion years ago, our early Universe was completely dominated by dark matter. However, as it ages, it is expanding much further out. The domination of dark energy thus automatically increases. Incidentally the best way to explain dark matter is that it is composed of particles that do not absorb, reflect, or emit light, so they cannot be detected by observing electromagnetic radiation. Dark matter is material that cannot be seen directly. In fact dark matter may account for the unexplained motions of stars within galaxies..."

He could see Jones and the other students absorbing the information. They had well and truly sent him off at a tangent, but their curiosity was gratifying.

"Professor," said another one of the students. "I wanted to ask you something about black holes..."

"Sure Graham, go ahead!" So much for the planets of the Solar System, he thought to himself, "but let's make this the last question for today please..."

"Thank you Professor... Tell me, if a black hole is sitting at the centre of its galaxy, do you believe that it distorts the fabric of the universe around it?"

"Yes Graham... it leaves a dent in this sheet of spacetime from which nothing can escape... this includes even light. Funnels made by the black hole twisting the spacetime fabric suck up particles which are accelerated by electric currents before being driven out into space as beams of radiation and of course, charged particles... As you know many black holes start life as stars... Stars spend their entire stellar life resisting what is known as gravitational collapse. In other words their huge mass means that the gas is constantly pulled towards the core. Instead of collapsing down, atoms collide and fuse... As a result of this stellar activity, explosive atomic energy is released. Radiation pushes outwards against gravity holding the star open as a glowing ball of gas. As a star grows old, heading towards stellar death, or entropy, more of the atoms are fused thus creating heavier elements. Eventually the fuel starts to diminish. Without the outward push, the balance is tipped in favour of the immutable force which is, of course, gravity. As a result the star begins to collapse... A dense neutron star or black hole is then formed. The curvature of spacetime inside a black hole is directed towards a single point. This is known mathematically as a singularity... Finally, some black holes spin at half the speed of light. Spinning black holes distort spacetime wrapping it into a swirl known as the ergosphere..."

He paused with a warm smile...

"Thank you Professor," said Graham eyes focused.

"That's what I'm here for. Okay, that about wraps it up. Now, for the remaining forty minutes please work on your assignments... You have exactly one week to complete them..."

He cut off and relaxed back in his chair, gazing at the bright-eyed students before him... Kirsten smiled at him meltingly, her blue eyes wide and admiring. Moments later, she became mock-business-like focusing on her work. Gregory's mind returned to Sheldon and his astonishing story of a metaphysical opening... Encapsulated in thought, everything around him seemed to fade into a blur as his mind worked away.

Later that day, Gregory found himself alone, seated in the dim-light of a large bar downtown. It was 8pm, dark... He needed some time alone, time to reflect more on Sheldon's incredible encounter and time to think about a potential move to Canada. He knew his wife Elaine wanted the change desperately despite his continual resistance... The bar resembled something from the 1950's, all polish and oozing class, with jazz music playing in the background... His mind flowed with the thread of the melody. On the rear wall was a large vid-screen. A weather report was being broadcast silently. Around him customers ate and drank, some nodding their heads jerkily to the music. A dating couple stood up and began to dance, skilfully changing steps as the music rolled. His head began to ache due to the constant hum of voices mixed with the bright clothing and the movement of bodies. Finishing his double-scotch with a gulp he stood up and walked out onto the night draped street. A strong cold wind galloped across the city fading into the night darkness. Above him hover-cars flashed across the sky, humming. On the street people moved around feverishly, chatting and gesticulating; most of Chinese and Japanese extraction. Neon lights flashed and flickered and pulsed red, orange and green. The scent of oriental food drifted warmly across the street. He stood for a time and watched the breaking crowds. People moved around like zombies getting in each other's way; confused and aimless people each lost in their own worlds. A few people glanced at him idly. Focused on home he hunched his shoulders and walked on passing a heavily crowded Japanese restaurant, a beehive of sound and activity. A section of the street was littered with squashed cigarette butts and debris. Within minutes, his silver hover-car, R1 was in view. With the press of a button the door flipped open, and Gregory gratefully clambered inside, latching the safety belt on...

"Home please, R1," he muttered hurriedly.

R1 rose from the ground, ascending higher and higher. The sky overhead was perfectly clear and ablaze with the familiar, friendly stars. Once in position at the correct altitude it began to glide away high above the city of Philadelphia. Almost immediately, the vid-screen buzzed into life. A face formed in the ripples of visual static. It gave out a distinctive hum as it cleared, and the face on the screen became as defined and sharp as could be.

"Everything okay?" asked Elaine elegantly perched on the sitting room sofa, the soft sounds of classical music, Vivaldi, just detectable in the background. A series of solemn, breathless chords framed themselves in his inner ear. The classical music was distinctly different to the jazz music he had been listening to. Both were equally appealing...

He replied, "Yes, I'm heading back."

"How long before you're home." She shot him a sexy smile.

"Around twenty minutes."

She waved, and with the other hand blew him a kiss. He smiled. Her face faded across the neat screen. He turned his gaze to the sea of colourful dots passing below; buildings, city life, a stir of chaotic urban motion. He licked his upper lip and consulted his chronometer. He then clicked on the entertainment vid-box. A documentary was showing a spaceship approaching Pluto's orbit. Pluto and Neptune were on the far side of the sun. He switched channel. Another documentary about space was being broadcast. The face of the ubiquitous Professor Francis L. Newton filled the screen.

In his usual sharp British accent he said, *'simply put, in astronomy, the interstellar medium is the material which fills the space between the stars, matter and radiation. This matter includes gas in ionic, atomic and molecular form, as well as cosmic rays and dust. In addition, it fills interstellar space and blends into the surrounding intergalactic space. The energy that occupies the same volume, in the form of electromagnetic radiation, is the interstellar radiation field. Approximately 99 per cent of the interstellar medium is composed of interstellar gas and of its mass, about 75 per cent is in the form of hydrogen, either molecular or atomic, with the remaining 25 per cent as helium with trace amounts of carbon, oxygen and nitrogen. Furthermore, the interstellar gas consists partly of neutral atoms and molecules, as well as charged particles, such as ions and electrons.'*

The hover-car dropped speed with a sudden jolt. It seemed to drag a little. He deactivated the vid-box and examined the read out of the hover-car's course across a small monitor. The AI system came to life and declared, "Sir, it's too late..." Its words were swallowed up! Before he knew it the hover-car entered a strange opening in the sky... a blue sphere of light soaking up energy through thermoelectric currents... Cold terror struck him hard. This can't be, he thought! R1 had no time to adjust... The hover-car began to bounce around. The bright penetrating blue light shone, so intensely it was blinding, a sting to his eyes. The light began to flicker and he felt a tremendous weight gather over him. Actinic blue flames flashed across the hover-car throwing high energy particles and electromagnetic fields about with care-free abandon. Fusion radiation moved wickedly through his body...

A loud roar followed. He closed his eyes tight and tried to ignore the sweat streaming down his face. The hover-car moved violently, rocking from side to side. Then suddenly it stopped. He opened his eyes and found himself gliding above a desert in the midday sun... The hover-car began to shake again, and he jumped as R1 blasted out, "Prepare for an emergency descent Sir..." It fell like a stone for twenty meters, but managed to regain some semblance of control, shaking and tilting violently but gliding towards the ground in a non-lethal trajectory. Gregory almost lost consciousness, the seat belt his saviour. He was dizzy, disoriented. As R1 reached the desert landscape it crash-landed safely with a minor bump, all systems fading into silence, a deathly silence. And in that little space of silence, Gregory's dazed brain clutched desperately for sanity, for steadiness.

He looked around and realised that he was stranded in a desert. Still half dazed, he began to regain his mental balance and awareness. Then it hit him... the blue light, the sudden change of scenery, the sudden shift from night to daylight. It could not be, he thought, but the reality of his predicament pummelled his mind into acceptance. The unknown was a terrible place...!!! Perhaps this was one of those alternate realities he'd discussed with Sheldon. The chances of it happening to him went against the laws of probability and statistics and yet it had happened. The evidence was staring him in the face! He felt awed, humbled and disbelieving. He leaned forward. His eyes narrowed. In an icy tone he asked, "R1, where are we?"

"Sonoran Desert Sir, Arizona… Sonoran Desert Sir, Arizona," on the third repetition R1's voice became distorted, slow, and sluggish, "Sonoran Desert Sirrr, Arizonaaa... It shut down. A strange mechanical sound followed... then total silence. R1 had ceased its mechanical function. It was completely inoperative.

In desperation he yelled, "R1," give me the exact location? R1...!"

It was no use. His dependency on R1 had had come to an abrupt end. The highly complex AI system had stopped operating. With this realisation, Gregory, his face dripping with sweat, flipped the door open and stepped out on to the soft shifting desert sand. Dazed and reeling as a result of the metaphysical switch from one dimension to another he glanced towards the horizon, the sudden displacement tearing through his mind. Miles of burning sand engulfed him in all directions.

The idea of being stranded in the desert was unthinkable so he didn't think about that. Instead, beneath the blazing desert sun, he began to think about his discussion with Sheldon. At the time it had been for him a fascinating intellectual discussion. It now seemed he might owe Sheldon some sort of apology. He still couldn't quite believe that he'd travelled into another world, another dimension. All events suggested so. There was no other explanation.

He grew agitated. Taking a deep breath, he filled his lungs with the dry desert air. The heat was intense. Particles of sand swirled through the vast wilderness without limit or end. He was rubbing his eyes, attempting to adjust to the light when he became aware of a large hover-jet gliding slowly across the clear blue desert sky. He thrust his head forward and eyed it coldly, filled with a sense of both fear and awe, almost losing his balance. His eyes remained fixed on the glistening white object. Then from beneath the jet, a smoke-tinted dome of light was ejected from an opening. Almost like a waterfall, it fell with a whoosh and within seconds it had enveloped Gregory. His eyes began to water, a strange, acrid smell tearing at his nostrils. He had no time to move, react, or think. The light swirled around him and lifted him high into the air. He began beating his fists in the air as if to somehow free himself but a wave of dizziness struck him and he stopped. Immersed in the light he was almost magnetically pulled into an opening in the bottom of the large hover-jet. Everything went black...

He awoke lying on a bed surrounded by five young men all dressed in matching luminous white uniforms. There was a swelling undertone of whispering among them. His gaze swept the blur of faces; none he recognised. He was in a chamber with grey walls and someone had dressed him in a white robe. Torn with bitter confusion he went to open his mouth in protest but failed. A minor irritating sting on his right arm suddenly drew his attention to some tiny puncture marks and his indignation turned to fear.

"There's something different about this man," muttered one of the young men jerking a thumb in his direction. Another said, "Isn't incredible to think that the brainstem actually is the thing that keeps us alive. It performs so many automatic functions like breathing, heart rate, waking, sleep cycles. It acts as a relay centre connecting the cerebrum and the cerebellum to the spinal cord." In his enthusiasm he missed the rolling eyes of his colleagues.

The five unknown men gathered around Gregory and wheeled him out of the chamber into a brightly lit room. Even in his dazed state, Gregory could still recognise students when he saw them. He looked around as far as he was able and saw people in lab coats wondering to and fro. Across the wall he saw a banner. It read: Commanding Forces research lab and medical training.

"Right, let's proceed with the special brain scan," said a voice, made sharp and brusque with efficiency. Gregory just caught sight of his name badge proclaiming him to be Dr A. Litbarski head neurologist. He rubbed his moustache, his eyes gleaming, as he launched into an explanation of brain anatomy and physiology.

"Now, the brain can create structures in up to 11 dimensions as we will see with this subject. The brain is full of multi-dimensional geometrical structures operating in as many as 11 dimensions. I'll use algebraic topology, a branch of mathematics that describes the properties of objects and spaces, regardless of how they change shape. Algebraic topology provides mathematical tools for discerning details of the neural network both in a close-up view at the level of individual neurons and on a grander scale of the brain structure as a whole. Algebraic topology is like a telescope and microscope at the same time... By connecting these two levels, we can discern high-dimensional geometric structures in the brain, formed by collections of tightly connected neurons and the empty spaces between them. These empty spaces or cavities seem to be critically important for brain function. Furthermore, I've found that groups of neurons connect into cliques, and that the number of neurons in a clique would determine its size as a high-dimensional geometric object. There are literally tens of millions of these objects even in a small speck of brain tissue, up through seven dimensions. In some networks, we even found structures with up to 11 dimensions. Remember human brains have approximately 85 billion neurons, with multiple connections from each cell webbing in every possible direction, which in turn forms the vast cellular network that somehow makes us capable of thought and of course consciousness. Soon we will have a digital brain model..."

Dr Litbarski paused. He reached over for a syringe. Holding it expertly he gave his subject a shot in the right bicep. Gregory instantly felt weak and dazed and the doctor's face leaning over him began to fade. The ceiling started to swirl into a vortex of eventual blackness. He drifted into the dream world, where he was assured by the droning voice of Dr Litbarski that his dreams were nothing more than vivid, sensorimotor hallucinations with a narrative structure.

He awoke to find himself sitting in a large chair. He drew a cautious breath and gazed up to see a man standing before him. The man was dressed in a black uniform that fitted tightly around his slim torso. His eyes were like two tiny spheres of utter blackness and they glinted with harsh detachment. He was bald, pale in colour, clean shaven and he stood with an air of authority. Fear surged through Gregory, penetrating to his core. He battled to remain calm. They looked at each other for a short time without uttering a word. It was as if they were speaking to each other by the transference of thought impulses. As if they both knew what was nestled in the other's mind. But Gregory felt a much needed glimmer of triumph that it was not he but the other man who broke the silence.

"I'm Heinrich C. Dremmler, head of Commanding Forces."

"Where am I? Which city...?" Gregory asked, anxiety beading his face with sweat.

"You're in the central building of the Commanding Forces here on the outskirts of Los Angeles."

"What year, what date?"

"2099, January 2nd."

Gregory worked the dates in his mind. They correlated fine with his own reality. But the rest didn't... Then he remembered the blue light, the desert, the large hover-jet, the light that had lifted him into the belly of the jet, almost supernaturally. All that was enough to confirm that he had indeed entered another dimension.

"Who are you?" snapped Heinrich.

Gathering his courage, he answered, "I'm Gregory, Gregory Seymour, a scientist, an astronomer."

"What were you doing off limits? You were out of your jurisdiction. The deserts are used for highly dangerous experiments and training, especially the Sonoran Desert in Arizona. You know the law. The Governing Fathers have made it very clear. And why is your brain clear of the encephalic nano-chip?"

Gregory's blank face prompted further explanation.

"As part of your medical checks, you were utilised as part of a training course for the up-and-coming doctors within the Commanding Forces. Your brain was scanned to its max. No chip was seen nor detected. Why? It's the law. Every single living human has a chip inserted into their brain. The only people who are exempt are people that function within the Commanding Forces, soldiers, doctors, scientists, etc. We are the protectors of our Governing Fathers... part of the elite but you are not."

Gregory froze, his mouth dry. He could not quite believe what he was hearing. All this was further proof that he was in another dimension. A parallel dimension that was drastically different to the world he had known. He needed to discover more. Two vital questions hovered is his mind and he wanted answers.

"You speak of these Governing Fathers. Who are they?"

Heinrich's eyes widened...

"Had we not scanned your brain, I would have thought that you were either mad or suffering from damage to the region of your brain that regulates memory. Given that your hippocampus and your limbic system were given the all clear, I remain perplexed."

"I'm asking you this question because I'm not of this world."

Heinrich gazed deeply into his eyes and stepped closer to him.

"What are you saying?"

"This may sound ludicrous but somehow I have stepped into a parallel dimension. There are drastic differences between my world and here."

"Mr Seymour, this story of yours is absolutely absurd to say the least."

"No," snapped Gregory in desperation. "Please listen to me. I'm not of this world. I was catapulted into an alternate dimension, a parallel dimension, some kind of space-time continuum. You have to believe me."

"Okay Mr Seymour, if you insist on this story, so be it. For now I'll let it go, as crazy as it sounds. We shall soon discover the truth."

"Good," said Gregory. He felt encouraged enough to push his luck a little bit further. "Now, please, I ask you, who are the Governing Fathers?"

Heinrich turned and paced around the room hands behind his back, eyes perplexed.

"The Governing Fathers are the leaders of the world... a group of brilliant minds, a group of philosophers who control our world, our system. They are our gods... the only real power. But every child knows this."

"In my reality, in my world, there is no such group, no such system... Tell me about these nano-chips?"

Heinrich sat and looked intensely at Gregory's face for an uncomfortable moment. Finally he shrugged, as if to say it could do no harm and said, "Ever since

58

the Great Crisis some forty years ago, when economic and ecological collapse reduced the world's population, nano-chips have been used to monitor the minds of man. Inserting these chips into the brain, has given us the ability to monitor all thought and emotion. We can now, literally, read people's minds via this technology."

A few seconds of silence fell...

"Hacking into the human brain required us to decode the logic of neurons, and this we have achieved, thanks to the brilliance of our scientists. As a result, crime has decreased substantially and can even be prevented. In a sense we can see into a potential future."

He paused for a short moment. Then continued...

"Remember the mind is a power in the universe. Take control of the mind, in turn you take control of the man. The mind is the key to the man. Once the chip is implanted it has the capacity to store all cephalic data, every single thought and emotion. Then, via signals which are sent out from a satellite in space, all the stored information on the chip, all thought and emotion, all brainwave activity is collected. It is then registered on a giant computer. From there, special agents who form a division within the Commanding Forces, monitor everything..."

"In my world, this was something that was being discussed amongst the elite within the realms of AI... transhumanism, but it never developed into a reality."

Another pause dragged on as both men eyed each other...

"Mr Seymour, most humans are arrogant, selfish, without honour and will do anything to attain higher status. We consider ourselves to be highly evolved, but in certain respects, man remains nothing but a great ape, a proconsul erectus. The duality of man, this good and evil cycle if you like, places us into a unique category in the animal kingdom. Total control is the only way to steer mankind, otherwise chaos emerges as we have seen from times past. Placing these chips into the limbic system of the brain, means we have a world that is monitored and controlled. Our Governing Fathers lay out the rules and our futures."

Seconds of silence fell...

"Furthermore, the limbic system is the part of the brain that deals with mood and of course, instinct through the amygdala which is responsible for emotions, survival instincts, and memory and can activate an automatic, instinctive reaction."

"So a mind controlled society... a bunch of organic robots!"

"Yes Mr Seymour, organic robots. As I have just said, there is no other way. It's the only way to steer the world. But in compensation we have given the people a god-like gift."

"A gift...?"

"Yes, the mind-controlled population has access to unlimited knowledge, literally."

"What do you mean?"

61

"A fusion of brain and AI. Basically advances in nanotechnology, artificial Intelligence and computation, have resulted in the development of a 'Human Brain – Internet Interface' that connects neurons and synapses in the brain to vast internet-computing networks in real time... It links brains and internet-based data storage through the intercession of nanobots positioned at strategically useful neuronal junctions. Immediate access to information and data thus becomes possible without the need for internet cables and computers. Minuscule robots are injected into the human vascular system through which they navigate their way to the brain. Once there, the bots position themselves accordingly inside individual cells. Once in position, they are induced to wirelessly supply 'synaptically processed' and encoded human-brain electrical information via auxiliary nanorobotic fibre optics. In short it allows people to obtain direct, instantaneous access to virtually an endless, unlimited amount of knowledge. We now have a world of global super brains."

Gregory wiped his forehead and said, "Again, this was a project spoken about within Transhumanism and AI extensively. But in my dimension, my world, it never came to pass. People fought the idea, and as a result the whole project died on the table."

Heinrich did not reply. He continued to gaze at him as if trying to read his mind.

"So, what now...?" asked Gregory. His eyes felt red and itchy with fatigue.

"Well, the next logical thing to do is establish the truth. Test this bizarre story of yours, of parallel dimensions... alternate realities."

"How can you test such a thing...?" Gregory asked grimly. "It is what it is, believe me. You just have to accept what I am saying."

"Mr Seymour, for a scientist, your thinking is somewhat limited! If what you are saying is true, you have a counterpart, surely... There must be another you in this dimension."

"Yes, based on theories of metaphysics, of course," replied Gregory. But he's probably crossed over into my world or perhaps another."

"That doesn't matter..."

"What do you mean?"

"Mr Seymour, we have the records of everyone, as I have just explained in some detail... We have several ways to find and locate the other you and we shall with immediate effect... If there are records of another Gregory Seymour, then it proves your case! This is the only way that I can substantiate your claim."

Soon after, Gregory found himself standing in a large chamber. His right hand had been precisely placed on top of a device that ticked and hummed almost sequentially; the activation module apparently. The bright lights faded into darkness and he could only just make out Heinrich, seated beside him, legs crossed.

"Okay, Mr Seymour, it's an easy procedure from here. Look ahead."

Seconds passed and a hologram ballooned into existence. At first there was an oscillating haze of light. Then slowly it began to take shape triggered by the activation module. The form of a young brunette woman said, "Greetings! Please give the name and details of the person you wish to locate."

Gregory's eyes, for a brief moment, ached from the glare of the light. Although complete, the hologram wavered and altered. He said anxiously, cheeks burning red," Gregory Seymour, university Professor of astronomy, Philadelphia, married to Elaine Seymour, address 72 Creek Wood."

Within seconds of relaying the information the hologram faded. Then almost instantly another hologram came into existence, followed by another; it was the other Gregory, his counterpart, with his wife Elaine. Although an identical copy, Gregory noticed something different in the eyes; the expression was not quite the same. As for Elaine, it was her, identical in every way, except for the strange glow that was in her eyes too, something he couldn't make sense of but was undeniably there.

Heinrich stood up, mouth gaping. He rubbed his head in awe and stepped closer to the holograms as if he were seeing a ghost. The face of the woman did not return but her voice did.

"Gregory Seymour, Professor of Archaeology, Montreal, Canada, married to Elaine Seymour, address 118 Bergamot Place, both deceased in hover-car crash. Date: 2099, January 1, yesterday."

Gregory snatched his right hand away from the activation module. Instantly the voice of the woman and the holograms faded into obscurity. The bright lights of the chamber were suddenly restored. He was speechless... In this reality he had ceased to exist. Killed in a hover-car crash yesterday with his wife in, ironically, Montreal the place he had refused to go in his own reality, the place Elaine had so desperately wanted to move to. He thought hard, considering the other variable. In this world he had worked as a professor of

Archaeology, not astronomy. He now wondered about his friend Sheldon but pushed the thought aside. Heinrich was standing in front of him with a peculiar look on his face but his eyes were shining.

"Mr Seymour, what I have just seen transcends belief. You do indeed seem to be speaking the truth... I suppose this explains everything."

"Yes, it does," replied Gregory. "And now that you know, there is only one thing remaining, help me find a way back. I don't belong here. This is not my world. If I am to have any chance, I must return to the desert and repair my hover-car. From there all I can do is hope that I encounter that doorway again and re-enter the world I left behind. You've got to help me..."

Heinrich raised his brow, studying his guest intently. He said, "You will remain here with us for now. You will be washed and well fed, placed in a special unit with a bed, a computer. I need to speak with my superiors. Then we will figure out what to do next..."

Gregory sat alone in his room in front of a computer, the door locked and guarded by one of the soldiers of the Commanding Forces. He had eaten, and washed. His feet rested on the white stone floor. He had spent hours contemplating much, his mind a twisting, turning web of thoughts. He pictured his wife Elaine, his own predicament, the death of his counterpart. His fear had been somewhat nullified by cold curiosity and deep scientific intrigue. Although his ultimate goal was to find a way back, if there was a way back, he wanted to utilise his time to explore and see just how much he could discover about this alternate reality. As a man of science, research came naturally. With brisk fingers he began to type, searching out all the latest scientific breakthroughs, transhumanism and the latest achievements in technology and engineering. His eyes scanned the screen rapidly but nothing jumped out.

In terms of science, technology and engineering, everything that had been accomplished in this reality had been accomplished in his reality too; a total parallel, no variables in that sense. Then a section on the newly built space elevator caught his attention. This was different. He read:

'The space elevator – a planet to space transportation system; a giant structure rising from the earth and linking with a satellite in geostationary orbit, now in operation, electrically powered. Location: Pacific Ocean, near the equator.'

It had been constructed at sea, for safety reasons of course, he thought. He read on:

'The main component is a cable or tether anchored to the surface and extending into space. The design permits vehicles to travel along the cable from a planetary surface directly into space without the use of large rockets. The space elevator consists of a cable with one end attached to the surface near the equator and the other end in space beyond geostationary orbit, altitude 35,786 km.'

This was spoken about much in his world regarding space tourism but it had not become a reality yet, but it had here in this other dimension. He considered the science, the physics... the competing forces of gravity, which were stronger at the lower end and the outward-upward centrifugal force, which was stronger at the upper end, would result in the cable being held up, under tension, and stationary over a single position on Earth. His eyes returned to the screen and he read on...

'The cable material is made from carbon nanotubes.'

He suddenly wondered how it would deal with the problem of debris in outer space and potential meteor strikes. The cable would have to be very strong in order to absorb heavy potential impacts, he thought. Then he considered the most crucial advantage of having a space elevator. It would allow you to put things into orbit very cheaply. Rockets are expensive and limited. You had to expend a lot of energy to launch a relatively small payload. The space elevator, would not only require less energy but in principal, you could also reclaim energy during the elevators descent.

He considered the science involved again... as an astronomer it came naturally to him... You put the base of the space elevator at the equator, as they had done. Then at the top of the elevator you put a station or counter weight above geostationary orbit. That would balance both gravity and centrifugal force and allow the elevator to be held up under tension. From the station you could then launch space missions or use it as a base of operations to construct space stations.

Next he considered the fact that space elevators could also be built at the equators of Mars and the moon as part of future colonies on those celestial bodies. Gregory wanted to discover more. He found it fascinating that in this reality they had achieved an incredible accomplishment in terms of science and engineering, but he got side-tracked when he came across the following:

'The new Brain Implant made of needle-like electrodes penetrates the surface of the cortex and reaches the nerve cells that activate sight. The neuroprosthetic device allows blind people to regain functional vision, navigate and recognize objects. A

blind man was able to see for the first time and recognise letter shapes generated by arrays of electrodes implanted in his brain. The new implants are placed in the visual cortex.'

Again, this was something that had been talked about in his dimension and the necessary breakthrough was very close, but it had not yet been achieved in its totality, as it had here. He researched further articles.

'Quadcopter drone on Titan,' leaped out from the pages. He read: *'Quadcopter now on Titan alongside mothership. The drone has been operating above the moon's surface, taking various samples. When the drone's charge is low, it will return to the mothership to recharge. It also transmits all data obtained to Earth via the mothership. It has taken high-resolution pictures while collecting many samples of liquids and soil.'*

Incredible, he thought. A parallel dimension and yet so many differences in terms of advancement in certain domains. In his reality they were nowhere near even reaching Titan. This was truly groundbreaking in the field of robotics. He searched on and moments later read:

'Revolutionary Rocket Invention - the fusion rocket thruster... The unique design of the plasma thruster has enabled spacecraft to travel to distant planets much faster. The rocket uses magnetic fields to shoot plasma particles – electrically charged gas – into the vacuum of space. This process is found throughout the universe but is most observable to humanity on the surface of the sun. When magnetic field lines converge there, before separating and then reconnecting again, they produce an enormous amount of energy. Nuclear fusion is the power that drives the sun and the other stars. It combines light elements in the form of plasma – the hot, charged state of matter composed of free electrons and atomic nuclei that represents 99% of the visible universe – to generate massive amounts of energy.'

Finally, he thought merrily. I have found something that we have accomplished technologically in my dimension too, the same rocket breakthrough. He read on...

'Orbital Space Hotel with artificial gravity... Guests of the newly constructed orbital space hotel in low-Earth orbit enjoy private space walks where the only thing between them and the universe is a faceplate.'

Great, I have found another technological invention that has been accomplished in my world, my dimension.

'The habitable space hotel in low-Earth orbit spins fast enough to generate artificial gravity for its guests. The ring-shaped Voyager Space Station with a diameter of 650 ft with 24 integrated habitation modules, each 65 ft in length and 40 ft in diameter, creates moon-levels of artificial gravity...' He was all too familiar with this.

Satisfied at last, Gregory decided he had researched enough. He stood up and walked slowly to the barred window and gazed up to the heavens, the trackless void. The moon shone brightly as it escaped the swirling night mists. A setting moon always looks tremendous, regardless of dimension, he thought. His eyes fixed on it; he pictured the corroded surface and thoughts began surging through his perplexed, fatigued mind. Then fear began to stir within him. What was to come? What would Heinrich and the Commanding Forces decide to do with him? How were they going to deal with this bizarre situation? He was a man from another dimension, an alternate reality. He didn't belong here. Was there a way back? His mind spun and twisted with these endless thoughts... Tomorrow he would discover his fate... He finally turned and made his way to the bed...

Morning filtered in through the window, nudging Gregory into consciousness. Outside there was wild activity and commotion and he slowly became aware of the sound of rustling and footsteps. He gazed up, dimly alert, and saw Heinrich standing near the foot of the bed with an armed soldier. The soldier was tall, blond and well-built; a deep scar marred his face. He gazed at Gregory in awe, almost in disbelief. Gregory realised that the soldier must be aware of his story, his journey into this alternate dimension.

Heinrich snapped, "Mr Seymour, your fate lies in the hands of our Governing Fathers. Everything regarding yourself has been relayed to them. No need for a thorough cross-examination. We will now meet with one of the members of the elite Fathers. He will decide your fate. It's a four hour ride by jet. We leave in an hour."

Condensing his scattered thoughts and perplexed mind into some semblance of rationality, Gregory rose from the bed. Bright sunlight shone through the window, sparkling across the white stone floor. He ran a shaky hand through his hair and looked straight into Heinrich's cold black eyes and said, "Listen, I need to try and find a way back. I need to get back to the desert and repair my hover-car. It's my only chance and that's slim at best. You must help me. I've done nothing wrong. You speak about the Governing Fathers determining my fate... for what? Surely the only thing left now is to help me, the best you can."

"Mr Seymour, the Governing Fathers lay out the laws, everything goes through them. We leave in an hour..."

Heinrich turned and walked out, the soldier following behind. The door locked with a click followed by a hum. Gregory stood there thinking hard. There was no way out. No escape. The meeting was going to take place regardless. Who was this man he was going to meet? What other surprises lay ahead? He had to be mentally prepared for the challenge. It was time...

The hover-jet was in motion gliding smoothly in the atmosphere. Gregory sat in the still cold silence wondering, thinking. Across from him, Heinrich sat sipping from a mug of black coffee. Beside him the soldier was running his fingers across the smooth metal of his rifle. Suddenly Gregory heard a faint sound. He turned to look out of the small window. A slender hover-jet, similar in design to the one he was now in, was moving along with them, keeping speed. Gregory figured it belonged to the Commanding Forces. The sleek black jet was inscribed with a symbol depicting a tiger and a sword. A minute later it drifted off east and slowly disappeared into the sky. He wondered why there was no sound coming from the control-room. There had been none since their departure. He also wondered why he had not seen the pilot or pilots entering. It was bothering him so he asked earnestly, "Strange, all this time onboard this hover-jet and not once have I heard a sound come from the control-room; nothing at all. It's as if we are the only ones on board, flying without a pilot."

Heinrich turned his head and said, "You are very intuitive Mr Seymour. There are no pilots on board this hover-jet. It's being piloted by what we call The Brain."

"What do you mean?"

"Nestled below us, inside the jet, carefully protected and armoured, there is a human brain lying in a tank of liquid with a thousand minor electrical charges playing over its surface. As the charges increase, they are picked up and amplified and fed into the relay systems."

Gregory could not believe what he was hearing. It sounded utterly psychotic, and repugnant. It made him uneasy. He wiped his head nervously. The hover-jet was coasting evenly in the hands of a Brain.

"This sounds surreal."

"It's the truth Mr Seymour." Heinrich smirked. "Brains have been transferred to function in this capacity several times. It was an experiment that worked well, as you can see. When body destruction takes place, death, we keep certain brains alive, the brains of all the top intellectuals. When the great minds of our world die, we keep them alive. So in a sense they are still living, operating without a body."

Gregory fought to hide his shock and asked, "Do all your jets operate this way?"

"No, just a few... Thrilling don't you think? Quite an adrenaline rush..."

Gregory started to realise that Heinrich had a disturbed side to his personality. This made him feel even more fearful and concerned.

"Mr Seymour, via vocal command I can speak to it and instruct it accordingly. Via this microphone, I can give it any instruction at anytime. And it obeys."

He held a black microphone in his hand. It was connected to his seat. Gregory turned his head away. He still could not quite believe what he was hearing. It sounded utterly sadistic and unethical.

He tried not to think about it. As long as we get there safely, that's all that really matters, he thought. Heinrich seemed confident enough. Then from his inner sense of chronology, Gregory guessed that around four hours had passed. They must be close to landing and in confirmation of his reckoning the hover-jet began a prompt descent. The metal floor throbbed dully beneath them. They were almost there. Green fields came into view. Far out in the distance he caught sight of a towering building which pierced the crystal blue sky. He studied its dim outline. Minutes passed and they were close to the ground. He could now see a huge white palace. He squinted. Another few minutes passed... they were there. As the jet landed a group of soldiers approached dressed in their black uniforms. One other, probably a technician also appeared. Heinrich, Gregory and the soldier stepped out of the hover-jet. The air was humid and hot. Beautiful fields surrounded the palace that lay ahead, an undulating expanse of green, verdant countryside. The soldiers stood in a line and saluted Heinrich.

One said, "Lord Sheldon is waiting Sir, as per your scheduled meeting."

Heinrich nodded once in acknowledgment. Gregory in turn went a pale white hearing the name Sheldon. Surely this wasn't his friend's counterpart, he thought. He would soon find out.

The palace was grand in every sense. Beautiful pillars filled the lobby. The marble floor gleamed and sparkled. Pictures hung on the walls in elegant frames, highly sophisticated pieces of art. Even the scent, the warm aroma of flora in the air was fit for a king. Statues were neatly placed in corners.

Gregory found that the splendour of the palace was somewhat calming, giving him a false sense of security which he tried to ignore. They entered a huge hall. No windows were visible. It was empty and bare, but beautiful in design matching the rest of the palace. The soldier remained outside standing in military fashion.

Closing the thick wooden doors, Heinrich said, "Mr Seymour you need to stand in the centre of the hall. Lord Sheldon will appear on the balcony above."

Gregory walked towards the centre of the hall which was marked out with a circle. Standing in the circle he saw words etched into the marble floor beneath him, Gnothi Seauton. He knew the meaning, Know Thyself, attributed to the Greek philosopher Socrates in his world. The ancient Greeks of the past had obviously existed in this reality, just as they had in his. At least that's what the words indicated. After all it was a parallel dimension. There were going to be things that were exactly the same. This appeared to be one. He gazed up and saw the balcony that overlooked the hall. His heart began to beat hard. Who was this Sheldon? Was it his friend's counterpart? He waited, fidgeting in anticipation. Suddenly Lord Sheldon appeared at the balcony his eyes glaring down on Gregory. He stood like an emperor.

"Greetings, I'm Lord Sheldon van den Berg..." His voice was deep and polished. "You are Professor Gregory Seymour, scientist, astronomer."

Gregory's rigid jaw dropped and he stood there as if dead. He was transfixed. His flesh crawled. He shuddered and overcame the initial shock, somewhat but his face still twitched in sudden spasms. This was something he had anticipated given the fact he was in a parallel dimension but it was still hard to take in. It was indeed his friend's counterpart, Sheldon van den Berg. In his reality Sheldon was a good friend and a professor of psychology. In this parallel reality, he was one of the Governing Fathers, one of the leaders of the planet. He was dressed in a white one-piece suit, and he wore a long black cloak. The only facial difference was that he had a thick grey beard, well maintained, his blond hair was a little longer and his eyebrows were thin and sophisticated. Gregory could only stand and wait...

Lord Sheldon continued, "I have heard all about your mesmeric entry into this dimension Gregory Seymour. And your story has been verified and stands. Hard evidence suggests that as incredulous as it is, you are from another world, another reality. Heinrich tells me that your counterpart is dead and this is now certified. Thus, the facts I have here before me stray into the supernatural. You are the first man to enter our world from a parallel reality, at least as far as I'm aware. Many scientists have discussed this theory throughout the ages. You are living proof that it is not hypothetical but is in fact, a scientific reality, declared by your very presence."

"Yes," exclaimed Gregory, bubbling inside, still gripped with awe. "In fact, the truth is Lord Sheldon, I know your counterpart very well. In my world, my reality your counterpart, Sheldon van den Berg is a good friend, in fact a work colleague of mine, a professor of psychology..."

"Wonderful," muttered Lord Sheldon almost playfully. "It's an incredible thing to think that there is another me existing in another world, in another reality and that you know him as a friend. This makes our encounter here today rather extraordinary... very special indeed, don't you think?"

"Yes, Lord Sheldon, I'm still finding it hard to take in along with all the other details... So, the question now is what next...? Where do we go from here? What do you want from me? Now that everything has been established, surely the only remaining humane and ethical thing to do is to help me get back to my hover-car in the desert, repair it and give me a chance to find a way out, if there is a way out."

"Mr Seymour, do not forget, it is I who decides your fate and I have already made my decision."

Gregory's eyes grew wide... His heart began to beat fast. His mouth was dry. His future had been decided and he had little say in it. Lord Sheldon gazed deeply into his eyes...

"Mr Seymour, we shall take you back to the Sonoran Desert and we shall repair your hover-car but then the rest is up to you. We will give you a chance to return to your reality, if you can."

Gregory breathed out a huge sigh of relief... He had not seen this coming and had feared the worst. There was apparently some humanity in this man. He wondered whether subconsciously Lord Sheldon had developed a soft spot for him, given that his counterpart was Gregory's friend.

"Thank you, Lord Sheldon! There are no guarantees that I'll find that doorway back. Perhaps it will find me as it did before. My chances are very slim at best, but I must try. I don't belong here. I need to get back to my world, my wife, my friend, my reality."

But Heinrich it seemed had no intention of letting him go just yet. "Lord Sheldon," he intervened obsequiously, "why not examine the subject's brain via the Dome? We can see into his past and all the way up to the present. I'd recommend it before his release."

"An excellent idea..! His mind will be easy enough to probe. Not to mention it will give us an insight into his world."

For an instant a surge of anger and revolt swam viciously through Gregory. "I've already had my brain scanned. What more is there to probe?" he protested.

"Yes, I'm aware of that," Lord Sheldon snapped, "but this is a very special scan. We shall dig deep into your mind and unveil your life from your childhood right up to this present point. We will make buried memories come to life, scan your entire existence. You will experience weird sensations; see forgotten moments of your past. Mentally you will be forced to leap back across time, and see your whole existence spread out before you. At the very least we will get a glimpse of your reality through your mind. It should prove very interesting. There are advantages in it for you too. Seeing your whole life displayed before you will give you a deeper insight into yourself. When we are finished, you are a free man. Hopefully you will find that doorway back."

Gregory slumped and studied the words beneath his feet, Gnothi Seauton, meaning know thyself... The Psycho dynamics of emotion! Emotions, persona, subjective things which must be experienced! It seemed he was about to do exactly that. Lord Sheldon followed Gregory's gaze.

"Mr Seymour, the ancient Greek aphorism, Know thyself, is one of the Delphic maxims and was the first of three maxims to be inscribed in the pronaos, the forecourt of the Temple of Apollo at Delphi. Those great philosophers of ancient Greece laid out the foundations of philosophical thought, Socrates, Plato, Aristotle, and so on. This saying is fundamental to the development of man. In it lies strength.... Gnothi Seauton is etched into the ground beneath you, and you shall discover more of yourself after this experience. I should warn you, the psychological transition will be sharp."

The words of Lord Sheldon had now clearly confirmed that both realties had shared the same history regarding the existence of the ancient Greek philosophers and Gregory said, "It seems we share the same history..."

Before he could finish, Heinrich reached over and activated a switch that was fixed to the wall. There was a loud hum that lasted seconds then... a dome of light fell towards Gregory from the high elaborate ceiling above. His heart leapt in surprise and the tissues of his body drew tight as if he were standing at the centre of a vacuum. He was completely encircled within this large dome of translucent light that shimmered faintly, almost ghost-like, flowing sensuously around him. A strange grey mist enveloped him, swirling fantastically.

He coughed and waved his hands in order to eliminate the fog but failed. A strange feeling came upon him. He felt disorientated. He knew that he was physically still, yet within his mind he had a sense of tremendous velocity. It was as though his mind was whirling across unimaginable gulfs and his brain expanding. Gradually the grey mist faded into the air about him. He blinked and peered around, wondering what was next.

Within seconds his wondering was over as, across sections of the Dome, images of his life began to appear as if relayed onto a large vid-screen, clear, bright and as real and tangible as life itself. Scene after scene followed, Lord Sheldon and Heinrich looked on. Chunks of memory broke free and drifted away like calved glaciers.

First his birth was displayed and his early years as a baby, then as a child. A mix of different scenes lay fixed to the Dome's wall, scattered moments of his life; Gregory as a teen, in school, university, his family members. His wife Elaine now appeared; their marriage. Scene after scene after scene of varying moments and forgotten memories, tears, laughter and pain... Gregory's eyes switched to and fro, recognising different phases of his life.

Then Sheldon appeared, standing in his office at the university in Philadelphia chatting with Gregory. At this point, Lord Sheldon froze, almost in horror as he gazed hypnotically at his mirror image, his counterpart, as the scene shone brightly across the Dome's wall verifying Gregory's account further. He already knew that Gregory was telling the truth, it was all confirmed via the ever-reliable hologram locator; Gregory's counterpart was dead. This was further evidence, further proof... Further images, countless images continued to roll and roll all the way through his life; his journey into the parallel world, the desert encounter, right up to the present moment.

Forty minutes had passed and the procession of scenes ended abruptly. Gregory stood there exhausted, breathing deeply, sweat running down his forehead. Then suddenly, another scene popped into view.

Heinrich gasped. This should not be happening! It is against all operational parameters and it just should not be happening, he thought. He focused closely, aware that Lord Sheldon was doing the same. The fuzzy image, became clear, and bright. It was an image of Gregory, kneeling down. In his hands lay what could only be a bomb; small, square, silver and metallic. The location soon became apparent as the image enlarged and magnified. The bomb was being placed inside the palace, this very palace, in what looked like an abandoned room. Somehow, an image of the future had been mystically revealed. It was the first and only time it had happened. Heinrich's eyes grew wide in astonishment... The scene remained fixed on the wall of the Dome as if frozen in time...

Lord Sheldon could not believe his eyes either. Emotion roared inside, rage dominating, as he gathered his thoughts. Seconds later the image of Gregory faded and, with it, the dome of light that had enveloped him...

"Lord Sheldon," blasted Heinrich, anger blazing across his face. "This has never happened before. Somehow the Dome has revealed this man's future intentions. The Dome has become a future teller."

"Wait a minute," cried Gregory desperately, "the Dome is not working on a genuine system of prediction. He could feel his heart pounding and the hot breath of destiny on his neck.

Heinrich ignored his protests and continued, planting the seed, "This is a clear picture of the future, an event that will happen unless..."

"Yes," snapped Lord Sheldon, his eyes hot with fire. "I cannot believe what I have just seen. It seems to me that Mr Gregory Seymour has somehow had his mind scanned beyond the present moment. He is to be taken back to base and executed at once. We can stop this event occurring by eliminating the subject."

"Wait," shouted Gregory, chill perspiration leaking from his palms. "This is impossible. I'd never do such a thing. There's an error somewhere. I'm a scientist not an assassin. I can't be executed for something I have not done, regardless of what the Dome has shown you."

"Mr Seymour, everything is predetermined. Somehow the Dome has captured a future moment in time."

"Lord Sheldon, it's about free will; my free will versus determinism. Free will wins every time. Determinism is no long considered rational within philosophy. Please, give me my freedom and a chance to leave this world."

"Heinrich, take him away..."

Heinrich called out. The doors opened and the soldier stormed into the hall. He grabbed Gregory, pulling him away with, Heinrich monitoring them both closely.

The hover-jet was moving fluidly through the atmosphere, guided by the mystical Brain. They were an hour away from LA. They would soon be back. Gregory sat fixed to the chair, awaiting death; his tortured mind besieged with memories, memories that brought burning tears to his eyes. There was nothing to console him, only a desperate desire to return to his dimension and escape death. Then other memories came and they blazed and swirled within the deepest confines of his mind like an unquenchable fire.

He began to consider an escape once he was on land, but a get away from the authorities was going to be a complex task, not to mention getting back to the world he once knew. He looked out of the side window and gazed at the blurred landscape below. Out in the distance he noticed a line of cavities that stretched on to near infinity... The surface of the land was pocked with great gaping sores. Huge cracks formed from the constant movement of tectonic plates.

"Mr Seymour," said Heinrich cool and dispassionate. "You've nothing to fear. We terminate life quite ethically you know. A simple injection in the arm leads to a deep sleep and eventually death."

Gregory remained hushed, his eyes focused on the landscape below. The awful feeling of dread threatened to overwhelm him. But he fought it off and remained calm... He was going to fight till the end.

Suddenly the hover-jet started to lose altitude veering to the right. There was turbulence. It began to rock from side to side, tilting with sickening results.

"What's happening?" yelled the soldier his face pale with fright.

Heinrich raised a transmitter to his mouth and spoke urgently to the Brain, "Regain altitude, I said regain altitude."

For a moment Gregory bizarrely wondered whether the Brain was trying to help him. Perhaps it was aware of his predicament? Of course he had no way of verifying this, but it gave him a brief sense of comfort, even though deep down inside he knew that it was a wild, preposterous idea. He shook off the thought...

The hover-jet now started to nosedive heading towards the ground below. An alert signal was sent out to base. The Brain, as Heinrich had called it was malfunctioning. Gregory gripped his seat. Looking over at Heinrich and the soldier, all the confused emotions of the past day came bursting out as he yelled at them, "Death is coming to us all! So much for the Brain...! With all your advanced technology you've left our lives in the hands of a bodiless mind. Obviously no backup system..."

Heinrich and the soldier did not reply as they battled to remain calm, gripping their seats in fear. The bitter stench of dread was all that lingered in the eerie silence that followed. Gregory braced for impact as the hover-jet lost power and speed... The ground below grew nearer and nearer as the seconds passed. Then, impact!

With a loud bang the hover-jet landed sliding across a field, showering sparks all around and then it began to violently break apart. Gregory felt the brutal impact expressed across his head and body in blurred chaotic fashion. Then silence... a deep and total silence blanketed the destruction that lay all around him. The hover-jet was now nothing but a charred ugly wreck. Suddenly something hissed feebly, making him jump, complex mechanisms slowly dying, the dim sound fading into silence again.

Gradually Gregory's eyes started focusing further afield. Bright sunlight lit the horizon and beyond with divine beauty and majesty. But it was fading slowly... The hour was declared astronomically with mathematical precision and Gregory was relieved to be a witness to such certainty again.

Heinrich and the soldier lay dead. Gregory, it seemed, had escaped... his life miraculously retained. He lay awake in a field of green, his life preserved despite the thumping great crash. For a moment consciousness went – snatched away in an instant. Seconds later it returned.

He opened his eyes as his face was caressed by a gentle breeze that inspired hope. He caught sight of the sky above and shuddered and groaned. A burst of adrenaline surged through him, rousing him. His mind cleared. This was his chance to get away. Slowly he got to his feet, shakily making a frantic, hasty inspection of the wreckage, the hazardous leakage of fumes plaguing his nose; most unsettling. Metals oxidize, plastics rot! He thought as he stumbled backwards but he was beginning to regain his balance and strength. Trudging ahead he caught sight of the two lifeless bodies, Heinrich and the soldier. They were covered in blood, battered horribly by the harsh impact.

Minus a few minor cuts and bruises he was whole and amazed by the fact. Perhaps this was a sign he thought, a sign to suggest that he would make it back home, well, back to his dimension. It gave him a further desire to fight but his heart sank as a strange, sudden wind hissed around the wreckage and a silver hover-car suddenly landed in the green field with a soft touch-down. A door flipped open, a man stepped out and gazed over at Gregory, eyes curious and sincere. He was tall and slim, with brown hair, dressed in a one-piece white suit.

Gregory was struck speechless, paralyzed, his mind tumbling in freefall.... He snuck an inquisitive look at the newcomer, almost as if he was seeing a bizarre hallucination, but he knew it was real, solid. Gregory had been all set to flee but something in this man's countenance inspired hope and trust. He cried desperately, "Please help me Sir..." He stopped and stared, lost for the moment, eye-sockets heavy; his soul burning for help.

"Who are you...?" the stranger's voice was brisk and efficient.

"I'm Gregory... Gregory Seymour, a scientist..." He shivered convulsively staring helplessly.

"A scientist?" The man smiled; a gentle disarming smile. His eyes flickered, deep and calm.

Gregory nodded slowly. He was swallowed up by a sense of unexplainable tranquilly. He trusted this man.

"Interesting... Well you are lucky to be alive, Gregory." The man rubbed his jaw thoughtfully, looking at the two dead men, Heinrich and the soldier. "Tell me, why were you travelling with these men from the Commanding Forces? From your attire and the expression in your eyes I know that you are not one of them." He blinked, studying Gregory's face carefully.

Gregory cleared his throat, "Yes that is correct. However, it's a long story... In short I was going to be put to death by these men, the Commanding Forces..."

"How ironic... A horrible crash has ended up saving your life. Tell me Gregory, are you fixed?"

"Fixed? I don't know the term."

The man seemed slightly confused by Gregory's lack of understanding. "Have you been implanted with the mind-controlling nano-chip?"

"No, be sure about that."

The man looked surprised and said, "How did you manage to evade the authorities? I thought I was the only one that had."

"Look it's a long story..."

Seconds of silence stretched between them, then the man came to a decision and gestured towards his hover car.

"Very well... Get in quick, the rescue team will be arriving here shortly, regardless of the fatalities. As long as you are, as you say, free from the nano-chip, they won't be able to locate us...come."

Gregory staggered towards the hover-car. Once in and seated they ascended into the atmosphere moving smoothly. Gregory sank back and closed his eyes in search of some rest as the hover-car turned on a radical slant heading into the horizon....

Darkness had descended. It was night and they were inside a small apartment, high up located in downtown Los Angeles. Gregory had washed and changed into some fresh clothes that had been given to him by his rescuer. The clothes were slightly baggy, but fairly comfortable. Leaving the bedroom, he entered the living room where the other man waited. Grey, silky patterned walls surrounded them.

"Take a seat Gregory," said the man.

Sitting on the sofa, Gregory said, "I appreciate all your help. Had it not been for you, I don't know what I would have done. Tell me, who you are?"

The man smiled reassuringly and replied, "My name is Jacque Descartes. I'm a computer scientist by trade. More to the point, and very much to your advantage, I'm anti authority, anti the Governing Fathers and, anti the Commanding Forces."

This made Gregory's eyes light up.

"In fact I'm the only man on this planet that does not have his brain monitored like a rat... at least that is what I thought until I encountered you! It was purely by chance that I witnessed the crash from above during my flight home. Curiosity got the better of me, and on landing, I inadvertently encountered you, the bright enigma."

"So, it was curiosity that lured you to the scene of the crash?"

"What else? I knew that the hover-jet belonged to the Commanding Forces from its unique structure and the distinctive seal, so naturally I was glad, certainly not concerned. Tell me, how is it you are free from the nano-chip?"

Gregory swallowed hard, rubbed his eyes and replied, "Jacque what I am about to tell you may sound unbelievable. In fact, you will probably consider me a mad man. But please be sure that I am not insane but very rational as you can see from our discourse. So please indulge me with your full trust, as inconceivable as what I am about to say may sound." He paused, and then blurted out... "I'm free from all forms of mind control because I'm not from this dimension."

Jacque scratched his forehead, failing to suppress the disbelieving smile that was forming across his face. "I'm sorry? What do you mean?"

Gregory tried again.

"Jacque, I'm from another dimension, a parallel dimension... an alternate reality."A few tears started to burn in Gregory's eyes. "This is not a theory but a fact my friend. I'm now looking for a solution... a way out of here... a way back into my world if that's even possible, given the way I was bizarrely catapulted into this dimension."

"Look metaphysics was never my strong point but what you are saying sounds ludicrous."

"Jacque, please hear me out... Does a mad man speak with such clarity? What I am saying is true. I've been catapulted into an alternate dimension, a parallel dimension, some kind of space time continuum."

Gregory's eyes began to flick from left to right, as if he were about to reveal the ultimate truth. Nervous sweat broke out across his forehead. He took a long deep breath and continued... "It happened this way... I was in my hover-car after a long day, journeying back home. Then suddenly the hover-car lost speed. Next, before I knew it, the hover-car entered into a strange opening in the sky... a blue sphere of light. A bright penetrating blue light that shone so intensely it was blinding. I closed my eyes. I found myself gliding above a desert in the midday sun... From there the hover-car safely crash landed. Moving fast through the sequence of events, I was then zapped up towards a hovering jet that hung in the atmosphere through an almost magical light source that swirled around me and lifted me into the air. I lost consciousness. Next I awoke on a bed surrounded by men. I was then taken into what seemed to be an operating room. Then a doctor came onto the scene. He put me to sleep via an injection. I then awoke on a chair and encountered a Mr Heinrich Dremmler Head of the Commanding Forces. From there we entered into a long discourse. He explained many things to me, like the mind control that dominates the world, the nano-chip, and the fusion of brain and AI... basically how advances in Artificial Intelligence have resulted in the development of a Human Brain Internet Interface that connects neurons and synapses in the brain to vast internet-computing networks in real time... He then spoke about the Governing Fathers, etc... He then asked why my brain is clear of the encephalic nano-chip. He then went on to say that I was utilised as part of a training course for the up-and-coming doctors within the Commanding Forces and that I'd had my brain scanned to its max and that no chip was seen nor detected. I guess this explains that blurred scene from when I awoke from that desert experience, that swirling light, the loss of consciousness and so forth... and found myself surrounded by those men... and then, next, taken into that operating room, then that doctor, then the injection, followed by sleep. It all happened there! Regardless, he wanted to know why I was free of that mind controlling chip because it was law. He went on to say that every single living human has a chip inserted into their brain. The only people who are exempt are people that function within the Commanding Forces, soldiers, doctors, scientists, etc... After answering his question in detail, I then explained who I was and what had happened. Logically sceptical, he wanted to discover the truth. I was taken into a large chamber in order to locate my counterpart, the other me, the other Gregory Seymour that metaphysically existed in this dimension. Via AI, holographic technology, the information was delivered. My counterpart the other Gregory Seymour was dead. So that you can understand a bit more, I'm a Professor of astronomy in Philadelphia, married to Elaine Seymour. My counterpart, the other Gregory Seymour who was confirmed as dead in this dimension along with Elaine Seymour my wife's counterpart was a Professor of Archaeology in Montreal, Canada. They were both killed in a hover-car crash on the 1st of January. In seeing this via AI, the hologram, my story was instantly validated, confirmed, thus Heinrich now knew that I was for real and that my story was authentic however incredulous. Next I was told that my fate lay in the hands of the Governing Fathers and that I had to meet one of the members. The next day, I was in a hover-jet heading to meet one of these men, a four hour journey escorted by Heinrich and a soldier. As the jet landed a group of soldiers approached. Stepping out the soldiers stood in a line and saluted Heinrich. Then one of them said... 'Lord Sheldon is waiting Sir, as per your scheduled meeting.' My face went pale white. A man called Sheldon is one of my best friends in my dimension. So given the sequence of events in this parallel world, I suddenly suspected that this Lord Sheldon might be his counterpart. Next I was inside a palace escorted by Heinrich and the soldier. It was a majestic palace as you can imagine. Stunning pillars filled the lobby and the marble floor gleamed and sparkled with exquisite beauty. I was then taken into a huge hall.

No windows were visible. I then walked towards the centre of the hall which was marked out with a circle. Standing there in the circle I saw the words etched into the marble floor beneath, Gnothi Seauton. I knew what it meant, Know Thyself. Next this Lord Sheldon appeared from a balcony above. And yes, as incredible as it was, it was indeed my friend's counterpart. My jaw dropped. In my reality Sheldon is a good friend, a professor of psychology. In this parallel reality, he was one of the Governing Fathers, one of the leaders of the planet, dressed in a white one-piece suit, and long black cloak. He said and I can remember the very words... *'I have heard all about your mesmeric entry into this dimension Gregory Seymour. And your story has been verified and stands. Hard evidence suggests that as incredulous as it is, you are from another world, another reality. Heinrich tells me that your counterpart is dead and this is now certified. Thus, the facts I have here before me stray into the supernatural. You are the first man to enter our world from a parallel reality, at least as far as I'm aware...'* I then explained that his counterpart in my world my reality was a friend, a work colleague, a professor of psychology. He was taken aback and said, again, I remember as if it were happening now... *'It's an incredible thing to think that there is another me existing in another world, in another reality and that you know him as a friend. This makes our encounter here today rather extraordinary...'* Now that everything had been established, I then asked what was next. Surely the only remaining humane thing to do is to help me get back to my hover-car in the desert, repair it, and give me a chance to find a way out... Against all the odds, meticulously recalled, he replied, *'Mr Seymour, we shall take you back to the Sonoran Desert and we shall repair your hover-car but then the rest is up to you. We will give you a chance to return to your reality, if you can.'* I was shocked. Then Heinrich Dremmler suggested that I have my brain examined via the Dome and see into my past all the way up to the present. Lord Sheldon thought that it was an excellent idea... They wanted an insight into my world, my reality via my memory bank. I was somewhat aggravated. And I let them no. I'd already had my brain scanned after my desert experience as I have already explained. This

Lord Sheldon went on to say that this was a special scan. And that they shall dig deep into my mind and unveil my life from childhood right up to the present point and that buried memories will come to life... Next there was a loud hum. It lasted seconds then a dome of light fell towards me from the high elaborate ceiling above. I was completely encircled within this large dome of translucent light that shimmered faintly, almost ghost-like. A strange grey mist then enveloped me. I was overwhelmed by a strange feeling. Then the grey mist faded. After that across sections of the Dome, images of my life began to appear as if relayed onto a vid-screen, clear, bright and as real and tangible as life itself. Scene after scene followed.... Countless images continued to roll all the way through my life... birth, childhood, my teen years, school, university, my marriage, my good friend Sheldon, forgotten memories, etc, then my journey into this parallel world, the desert encounter, right up to that present moment in time. Then incredibly another scene popped into view, something that went against all operational parameters, as if the Dome itself was somehow malfunctioning, that is, it should not be happening. In terms of this bizarre scene at first it was a fuzzed image, but slowly the blur cleared. Regardless, in short it was amazingly an image of me kneeling down. In my hands lay a bomb. The location was soon revealed as the image enlarged. I was placing a bomb inside the palace, that very palace itself, placing it in what looked like an abandoned room."

He paused for breath then continued passionately...

"So you see, bizarrely, a twisted, sick image of an obviously distorted future was revealed which has no truth attached. After all, I only have one intention, and that is to get back to my reality, my world, my wife. From what Heinrich and Lord Sheldon said, the Dome has never relayed a future scene before, this was the only time it has happened, meaningless as it was. And on that basis, Lord Sheldon sentenced me to death. I was taken to the hover-jet, then the crash happened, then you..." He faltered...

Jacque's demeanour had changed again. There was now a warm look on his face, one of calm acceptance, as if his whole train of thinking had suddenly switched tracks, a sudden metamorphosis and Gregory's anxiety began to fade a little.

"Gregory, I'm a man of science, like yourself, as I said, a computer scientist. At first, what you are telling me, it seemed ludicrous, however your explanation has snatched me away from the unacceptable, the unbelievable. Gregory Seymour I know you are for real... Perhaps I'm mad too." He smiled...

Gregory's relief was palpable. He now had a foundation, one to create a bond, a friendship that could potentially lead to a bizarre escape.

"Thank you, Jacque..." he said sincerely.

"But tell me, my new friend, how is all this possible?" asked his benefactor.

"I don't know how much you know but this is how we understand parallel dimensions to work. Mathematics is a powerful guide to the realms of reality. Mathematics leads us directly to the possibility that there are more than three dimensions of space as I, just by being here, have proven beyond any doubt. According to quantum mechanical hypothesis, universes are separated from each other by a single quantum event. Everything that exists can be at their own vibrational frequency. This leads to the infinite universe.... With this, universes can start repeating themselves because particles can be put together in many ways, many arrangements. Space-time is flat. The number of possible particle configurations and multiple universes would be limited to many distinct possibilities..."

"I see..." muttered Jacque in fascination...

"Now, approximately 13.8 billion years ago, everything we know of in the Universe was an infinitesimal singularity. Then in accordance with the Big Bang theory, some unknown trigger, a mechanism, caused it to expand and also inflate in three-dimensional space. As the immense energy of this initial expansion cooled, light began to shine through. Eventually, over the course of time the small particles began to form into the larger pieces of matter... planets, stars and galaxies, etc..."

A brief sharp silence fell...

"Now there are the five reasons why a multiverse is possible... Let's start with infinite universes. We do not know what the shape of space-time is exactly. One strong view is that it is flat and goes on forever. This would present the possibility of a vast number of universes being out there. But with that in mind, it's possible that universes can start repeating themselves. That's because particles can only be put together in so many ways. Next, bubble universes, eternal inflation. When looking at space-time as a whole, some areas of space stop inflating like the Big Bang inflated our own universe. Others however, will keep getting bigger, larger. Thus, if we picture our own universe as a bubble, it is sitting in a network of bubble universes. What is interesting about this theory is that the other universes could have very different laws of physics than our own, given that they are not linked."

He paused for breath then continued...

"Then we have daughter universes... Multiple universes can follow the theory of quantum mechanics. That is how subatomic particles behave. If you follow the laws of probability, it suggests that for every outcome that could come from one of your decisions, there would be a range of universes – each of which saw one outcome come into being. Next mathematical universes.... Mathematical universes in short explain that the structure of mathematics may change depending in which universe you reside... Finally, parallel universes... Going back to the notion that space-time is flat, the number of possible particle configurations in multiple universes would be limited to $10^{10^{122}}$ distinct possibilities, to be exact. Thus, with an infinite number of cosmic patches, the particle arrangements within them must repeat – infinitely many times over. This in turn implies there are infinitely many parallel universes... cosmic patches, exactly the same as ours, containing someone exactly like you as I discovered, as well as patches that differ by just one particle's position, patches that differ by two particles' positions, and so on down to patches that are totally different from ours. Anyway, in summary I'm living evidence that parallel realities exist. I'm standing in an alternate dimension as I have explained. Now, in this dimension, many things are largely the same in comparison with my own dimension, but there are still differences in terms of technological advancements and so forth..."

"Such as...?"

"This mind controlling nano-chip... This chip was spoken about in my dimension but never became a reality. Furthermore, this fusion of brain and AI which has resulted in the Human Brain Internet Interface was also spoken about in my dimension but never became a reality. The masses rejected it... In addition I have discovered that there is a newly built space elevator in this dimension. Again, spoken about in my world but not a reality... Next, I discovered that there's a neuroprosthetic device that now allows blind people to regain functional vision, navigate, and recognize objects. A blind man was able to see for the first time and recognize letter shapes generated by arrays of electrodes implanted in his brain. The new implants are placed in the visual cortex. In my world, the breakthrough was close, but it had not yet become a reality. Furthermore, I discovered that there is a Quadcopter drone on Titan taking various samples. In my reality we are nowhere near reaching Titan. I could go on. However, I did find two technological advancements that were made here that were also made in my world. They were the fusion rocket thruster and the Orbital Space Hotel with artificial gravity."

Jacque stepped in and said, "Okay, I understand Gregory. As I told you, I accept your story, as mystical as it all sounds. But now I must explain more about me and this mind-controlled world. Please indulge me.... As you have already discovered through your discourse with this Mr Heinrich Dremmler everyone has the nano chip implanted into their brains... barring me and of course you, given that you are not of this world. They never managed to fix my brain. During implantation I somehow managed to escape the authorities, and was not implanted with the nano-chip... You also told me that he spoke about how people's brains are connected to the internet...

Well, I'll add some additional information on both of these topics... I'm sure that much of what I'm about to address has already been told to you by that Heinrich, never-the-less, here goes... Nano-chips have been used to monitor the minds of mankind for some time. Man has become nothing other than a caged rat, a machine... Inserting these damn chips into the brain has given the Governing Fathers, the opportunity, whenever they desire, to monitor all thought and emotion. Basically, they can scan the brains of particular individuals at will. They can literally enter people's minds and read them via this technology. In terms of the actual science involved, well it all comes down to this... Hacking into the human brain requires decoding the logic of neurons as they fire and work symbiotically. As I'm sure you are aware, the brain is a complex network of approximately one hundred billion neurons. Different experiences create different neural connections which bring about different emotions and so forth. Depending on which neurons are stimulated, certain connections become stronger, more efficient, while others become weaker. This is known as neuroplasticity. Understanding the mechanics of neurons, neuroplasticity, and so forth lead to this mind invasion. Regardless, what it boils down to is that these hideous individuals have, rather expertly, achieved absolute mind control via these nano chips. They justify it by saying that crime has decreased and can even be prevented. My argument against it is that the biggest crime of all is to have a world of mind-controlled people, a world of organic robots. Man has been dehumanised!!! That's the greatest crime of all. So, their justification, in light of this, is totally flawed!"

He paused for a moment...

"In summary once the chip is implanted it stores all cephalic data. Then via signals which are sent out from a satellite in space, these signals collect all the stored information on the chip, all brainwave activity. The fusion of brain and AI? Well this is the cherry on the cake for them! As you were told, it links the brain and internet data through the intercession of nanobots positioned at neuronal junctions. As a result instant access to information becomes possible. Basically, minuscule robots have been injected into human vascular systems and they navigate their way to the brain. Once there and in position, that is inside individual cells, the bots are induced to wirelessly supply synaptically processed and encoded human-brain electrical information via auxiliary nanorobotic fibre optics. As a result people have access to an endless amount of knowledge... an apparent super brain is thus achieved."

"Yes Jacque, I understand, and I can see how immoral this all is... People have been dehumanised indeed."

"Correct... Now listen to this... Apparently these tiny nanorobots that travel inside people on a molecular level, protect your biological system and ensure that you'll have a good, long healthy life... Accordingly to the authorities, DNA robots can even destroy cancer cells. These programmed strands of DNA have the capability to move through the bloodstream, injecting blood clotting drugs into blood vessels around tumours, cutting off their blood supply. Personally I don't believe any of it..."

Gregory licked his lips in thought and said, "I wasn't aware of this Jacque. Please continue..."

Seconds of silence passed...

"Gregory, have you heard about the magical headset?"

"No I have not..."

"Well, there's a headset that allows you to edit your own feelings. Basically it's a brain-computer interface headset. The technology allows users to edit not only what they see, but their feelings and emotions as well. So, add the nano chip and the Human Brain Internet Interface to this and what you get is basically a robot... what was once a human being becomes nothing more than a machine... We call this transhumanism... mankind totally dehumanised! Back in times past they used certain techniques, creating order out of chaos, to arrive at this point. It was a slow progressive build up in order to reach the summit of total mind control. For example, in times past, they broke up and destroyed countless families using different strategic methods via the television and other media. This left children wanting and searching, brutally damaged and looking for that lost family bond through television which subjected them to mind-controlling tactics and games... Leaping ahead they even used the scholastic system, universities, etc to cleverly keep people under mind-control... the controlling power brainwashes its people via the academic system. They guide you through a scholastic tunnel which is as follows... read, write, we know and so forth... the end result... you come out with a worthless piece of paper, totally brainwashed, totally locked into their pathetic way of thinking. In short, the individual mind is repressed. Furthermore, digital immortality is a big thing here. A person's life data means a version of you could live forever which leads to brain uploading, the creation of digital avatars by an artificial intelligence platform that analyses personal data and correspondence."

"Yes, in my world, that was a big thing, but again the idea soon met its death as the masses rebelled against it on moral and ethical grounds."

"Well here it sadly dominates.... Indulge me a little more... The thought of a digital afterlife, the construction of a digital self, I find creepy beyond imagining. But the truth is that here they have built an application called augmented eternity. It lets you create a digital persona that can interact with people on your behalf after you are dead. It works like this... with enough data about how you communicate and interact with others, machine-learning algorithms can approximate your unique personality, or at least some part of it. It's being embedded into humanoid robots, would you believe."

"For sure," snapped Gregory. "The main complication with trying to create digital versions of the dead is that people are vastly complicated, like forty thousand personalities at once... regardless this is highly immoral."

"I couldn't agree more, Gregory... Now for the next part... Through cryogenics the actual practice of freezing people is taking place as we speak. They open up the chest of an individual through surgery. Access the major blood vessels of the heart, put you on an open circuit through a pump and a chiller system and remove as much blood as they can. They then replace it with what they call a cryoprotectant, which you can think of as medical grade antifreeze. They replace as much body fluid as they can with it so there's no ice formation, no ice damage and so forth... Once they have fully cryoprotected the cells, they plunge the temperature way down to minus 90 degrees C, very, very quickly. We are talking about super cold temperatures, cryogenic temperatures, where you could sit for hundreds, in fact, thousands of years and you'd be as fresh as when you started... so they say. They say they are just copying nature. For example, take a frog. During wintertime its whole being stops operating. The amazing thing is in the right season, its whole being re-starts in the proper sequence to let it live again..."

"Jacque, I'm somewhat familiar with this practice, that is, human cryogenics. It was spoken about in my dimension on multiple levels as an advance for the future, but it never became a solid reality, like so many other technologies it seems."

Jacque stood up with sudden purpose. The expression had changed to one of determination...

"Right..." he snapped. "Gregory listen to me carefully, we need to beat the system."

"What do you mean?"

"I want to put an end to this mind-control."

"But how...? That's surely impossible..."

"I'm going to fight this evil system... If I fail, I fail but I want to give it a go. And I want you to help me."

"But how...?"

"You know the answer. We need to plant a bomb in the Governing Fathers' palace... the central building... and we can do it together..."

A cold eerie silence fell. Jacques started pacing.

"Remember what you told me about all those scenes, those countless images of your life seen via the Dome... all your history displayed mystically, including your journey into this world. Then that final scene you told me about... that the Dome did something it had never done before...that future image of you kneeling, holding onto a bomb in the palace, the central building of the Governing Fathers. You placed it inside what looked like an abandoned room. Can't you see Gregory, this is your destiny. The Dome foresaw that destiny..."

Gregory was hit by the sense of fate, a sense of duty... Had that mystical Dome somehow seen into the future, a concrete future? Despite his initial rejection of it, was his destiny etched into the stars just as Jacque had indicated? Was this Jacque Descartes the cord that was to propel him to fulfil that destiny to bomb the Governing Fathers central building, the palace, just as the Dome had foreseen? Gregory understood the responsibility and the full implications even though he knew that beating the system was highly improbable. Kill for a greater cause; eliminate the enemy for a greater good... Those were the thoughts that suddenly plagued his stunned mind. Even though his prime objective was to get home, to return to his own dimension, even though that was seemingly impossible given the dynamics of his entry into this alternate reality, he suddenly felt compelled to assist Jacque. Beating the system was going to prove a colossal task. A cold, frightful chill surged through him. His heart began to beat hard... A strange feeling overwhelmed him but he remained composed...

"Jacque maybe this is my destiny, but bombing a building is one thing. We might be successful, but the truth is we will never beat the system. Its tentacles are stretched way, way beyond a building my friend. Never-the-less if you want my help I'm here and available, but remember, destroying a building won't stop this mind control, it is too deeply infiltrated. The power of the Governing Fathers goes way beyond a building my friend..."

"Yes, you are right Gregory. But I have no place in this world... I'm alone, totally alone. I live, I exist without the nano chip and all the mind-controlling gadgets, but I'm alone Gregory. I want to die a martyr. There's no point living like this in this twisted sick world. I'm tired my friend and have been for some time. I might as well fight, at least to some degree, regardless of the consequences. Thus, destroying a building may not result in the total elimination of mind control but it could be a catalyst for others to gather strength and fight as a result of my act. If the masses rebel, it could cause a revolution and even though my life might be taken along with yours we could be the martyrs that instigate a huge revolution, in turn waking up the masses. In time through our act of courage, many could wake up and fight. We have nothing to lose."

Jacque leaned forward anxiously waiting for an answer, but Gregory took his time, organising his thoughts.

"Jacque," he eventually said softly, "You are asking a lot. You say I have nothing to lose but remember, I have a wife and a normal life in my world, the one I want to re-enter however improbable. So, if I were to die for the cause, unlike you, I'd been giving away a potential life elsewhere... Not to mention that this is not my world. In a sense it is a semi-meaningless act on my part. However, given all the other facts, the Dome, etc, I will help you with this, given my predicament and that my chances of returning home are slim, at least the laws of probability and statics would suggest so. In one respect you are right; in this dimension I have nothing to live for, I don't belong here... so I will help you regardless of the consequences..."

"Thank you my friend... Remember Gregory, like you said there is no concrete way of you getting back to your world. So it's surely the logical decision to accept, as you have, this wicked destiny of yours, a destiny that will see you destroy the central building of the Governing Fathers just as the Dome has foreseen, to help me fulfil my task and hopefully see a revolution take place as a result. Remember my friend, whatever is meant to be, will be. If it is destined that you return home, it will come to pass regardless of your actions here. You really do have nothing to lose..."

Gregory looked at him unblinkingly.

"Yes, you are right Jacque..." He sighed and rubbed his head, deep-in thought for a moment.

"Jacque, I want to share something with you..."

"Sure, go ahead..."

"In my dimension, my reality, mind control takes place but nowhere near the level it does here, not even close. However I would like to share some history with you, history from an alternate dimension, my world... The mind control that takes place in my dimension has its roots in Munich, Germany, even though, as I have said, it has not reached the sick levels that it has here..."

He paused for a moment...

"Well, it all started with a Mr Adam Weishaupt. He was a German philosopher, a professor of civil law and later, canon law, and was the founder of a group called the Illuminati; basically a secret society. Weishaupt was born in Ingolstadt, Germany in 1748, a city in the Electorate of Bavaria, which is now part of my modern day Germany. Orphaned at a young age, his scholarly uncle took care of his education, and enrolled him in a Jesuit school. After completing his studies, Weishaupt

131

became a professor of natural and canon law at the University of Ingolstadt. Incidentally, does any of this connect with this reality?"

"No, I've never heard of such a person or of such a development. Things here evolved slightly differently in terms of mind control. We obviously have differences in our history, even though this is a parallel dimension."

"Indeed, it seems so... Well anyway, as I mentioned, this Adam Weishaupt became a professor of canon law. Convinced that religious ideas were no longer an adequate belief system to govern modern societies, he decided to find another form of 'illumination.' On the 1st of May, 1776, he founded the Illuminati. At the time, freemasonry was steadily expanding throughout Europe, within my dimension of course, offering attractive alternatives to freethinkers. Weishaupt initially thought of joining a lodge. Disillusioned with many of the Freemasons' ideas, however, he became absorbed in books that dealt with esoteric themes and notions, for example... the Mysteries of the Seven Sages of Memphis and the Kabbla, and thus decided to found a new secret society of his own. On the night of May 1, 1776, the first Illuminati met to found the order in a forest near Ingolstadt. There were five men bathed in torchlight. In the beginning, the order's membership had three levels. There were novices, minervals, and illuminated minervals. 'Minerval' referred to the Roman goddess of wisdom, Minerva, reflecting the order's aim to spread true knowledge, or illumination, about how society and the state might be shaped. Although at first the Illuminati were limited to Weishaupt's students, the membership expanded tremendously and soon included noblemen, politicians, lawyers, doctors as well as top intellectuals and some leading writers in my dimension like Johann Wolfgang von Goethe. In fact their main way of controlling people is through what is known as Ordo ab chao, which is Latin for order out of chaos."

"Yes, I'm fully aware of this saying Gregory. In this reality its origins lie in France. It was a French philosopher in 1771 named Jean Bossis who came up with the philosophical idea...order out of chaos. A group of Masons, wealthy noblemen from different countries took up the idea. It evolved throughout the course of time to bring us to this very point."

"Interesting but this did not happen in my dimension, my world. In fact, it was a German philosopher called Georg Wilhelm Friedrich Hegel who formulated this model of manipulation. He was born in Stuttgart, Germany in 1770... In my dimension, he is considered one of the fundamental figures of modern Western philosophy, with his influence extending to the entire range of contemporary philosophical issues, from aesthetics to ontology to politics..."

"Never heard of the man..."

"Well, let me give you a breakdown of his life so that you can understand a little bit more about how this mind control evolved in my world. Hegel was the son of a revenue officer. He had already learned the elements of Latin from his mother by the time he entered the Stuttgart grammar school, where he remained for his education until he was 18. As a schoolboy he made a collection of extracts, alphabetically arranged, comprising annotations on classical authors, passages from newspapers and treatises on morals and mathematics from the standard works of the period. In 1788 he went on to study philosophy and classics for two years and thus graduated in 1790. He then took a theological course. On leaving college, Hegel became a private tutor. This gave him leisure time for the further study of philosophy and Greek literature... Now back to the key point. Hegel developed a dialectical scheme that emphasised the progress of history and of ideas from thesis to antithesis and thence to a synthesis. It's called the Hegelian Dialectic. In other words, problem, reaction, solution... Basically you create the problem, get the reaction then provide the solution. In other words, they, the controlling powers, create chaos. Through the chaos that they intentionally create, the human spirit is broken. Man is frightened, left weak and wanting and is at his most vulnerable at this point. They then present themselves as the saviour with the solution. Man, being psychologically broken, in desperation, is looking for a saviour so he clasps the hand of the authorities and accepts their solution whatever it may be, thus accepting the changes that will come. They create new laws in order to control the masses further, restructuring society, economic systems, giving man a new way of living until total mind control is achieved, delivering their ultimate objective of total world domination..."

"Yes, Gregory I know this argument very, very well. Different histories in terms of its development, but ultimately the same result..."

"Yes correct... It was important to me to share this information with you so that you can understand how this mind control evolved in my world."

"Okay, but now enough talk, more action... Gregory, it's time to plant that bomb in the main palace... As we discussed, it won't lead to their ultimate destruction directly, but at least a sense of revenge will be accomplished. At least we will have sent out a message."

"Okay Jacque... but I have a question for you... How are we going to enter the palace? They have everything controlled, monitored. I was there. I've seen it. We will be killed well before we can even approach..."

"Gregory!" Jacques waved away his objections, "I have managed to steal three shipments of uniforms belonging to the Commanding Forces. All the crates are large; don't ask me how I did it, but I did. Thus, we are both bound to find matching sizes and we can disguise ourselves. Dressed in their uniforms we will enter unhindered and from there we plant the bomb. The rest will be history..."

"Do you think it will work?"

"Yes I do..."

"And the bomb...? Where is it?"

"It's in my bedroom ready to be unleashed."

"Where did you get it?"

"I built it myself, here, in my apartment. It took me three days to make."

"I see..."

ANTHONY FUCILLA

Again, Gregory's mind returned to the Dome that had mystically foreseen his future. At the time it was inconceivable, but now it appeared to be a confirmed destiny, defying the laws of time and physics. It was so obvious. All the current events brutally declared it. He had no choice. He felt compelled to see it through...

"So, when do you want to do it?"

"Tomorrow..! Remember they are looking for you Gregory. The longer we wait, the greater their chances of capturing you and in the process me. Even though I'm not a wanted man, technically speaking, I'm protecting you. I'll be seen as an automatic accomplice and branded a criminal, not to mention that they will soon discover that my mind is free of the nano chip... more consequences will then follow. So, let's get the job done tomorrow..."

Despite the import of what they proposed to do, Gregory managed to sleep the whole night through, finding comfort and much needed rest on the sofa. He stood, stretched, and took in a deep breath of air. As the early morning haze of half-sleep passed he gazed out of the window at the street below. He saw a mix of people moving around almost robotically like zombies, after all that's what they had become. Some were dressed in long stiff robes of mauve and gray, others in odd looking suits, all lobotomised and controlled. And yet at the same time via the Human Brain Internet Interface, they were walking super brains instantaneously having access to an endless, unlimited amount of knowledge. The steel micro-chipped jungle was a sight to behold.

He then made his way over to a small computer... He searched.... a new fact arose... a fact that in his alternate dimension had not yet come to pass, close but not quite. He read in computerised bold, *'Quantum information, Quantum communications... highly fragile quantum information...'* He digested the facts and read all the dazzling data. Regardless of his random metaphysical placement he was still a top intellect.

'Send, store and retrieve highly fragile quantum information. Internet of atomic nuclei in which they had injected a single particle encoded with quantum information. With every nuclei spinning in a different direction within the cloud, that is the internet, it is near-impossible to identify the particle carrying information. Using laser beams and a single electron, they can control the spins of the nuclei, restoring order in the cloud, internet, as a result they can detect the existence of quantum information with ease...'

Gregory absorbed the data silently... again... within his reality it was a thing to come, but here, within this alternate dimension it had been accomplished and had in fact become a solid reality. Then for a split second he thought about the randomness of quantum and linked it to the randomness of his journey. His mind returned to his primary objective... The bomb... after all, there was no concrete way of returning home to his reality given the facts and randomness of his entry into this world.

Jacque interrupted Gregory's research by walking into the living room holding a black bag. His eyes were filled with bitter determination. He almost appeared to glow with confidence, a metaphysical light, even though to the average eye it would go undetected.

"Gregory it's eight o'clock in the morning, it is time! Let us prepare and then we can head to the palace my friend. My hover-car is parked outside. Once dressed in the uniforms I seized, we will attempt the seemingly impossible, regardless of the consequences. As you know yourself, this is your destiny Gregory... what will be, will be... and if you are destined to make it back home it will happen, regardless."

The word destiny flooded Gregory's mind...

"Yes Jacque that I know. My longing to return home to my world cuts deep, but now it is time to fulfil my destiny here, in this alternate dimension... So let's do it..."

From the black bag he was holding, Jacque slowly, expertly, pulled out the bomb.

"This is it my friend... inside this small, square, silver, metallic box is a complex mass of wires and dials capable of doing some serious damage."

Gregory's eyes focused hard. It was the very bomb he had seen in that vision of the future granted him by the Dome. He still found it hard to believe. The shape and form was exact. It was small, square, silver and metallic.

"Jacque, that's exactly like the bomb I saw in that vision of the future, the one I placed in the palace, in the seemingly abandoned room. This is quite unbelievable."

"Yes Gregory indeed. And it will be you, just as in that vision, who plants it in the palace... I'll be there my friend don't worry. I'll be the watchman, the guard, but it is you, your destiny that needs to be fulfilled..."

Gregory's faced became hard as he pictured that very moment...

A cold hour swept by. Both men had successfully found matching sizes and were dressed slickly in the Commanding Forces distinct black uniform, with boots, ready for their mission, a task of immense proportions. As they left the apartment and made their way over to a large blue hover-car, Jacque gazed around, examining the street carefully like an owl. Across his shoulder was the black bag, nestled inside, the bomb. The pressure was immense and he knew that the Commanding Forces would be out looking for Gregory; after all, they had the world in their hands, these puppet masters...

People roamed the street, mind-controlled zombies strolling by robotically in the bright morning sunlight, almost unaware of their presence. Jacque put it down to the fact that because they were dressed in the black Commanding Forces uniform, people were fearful of them. He focused. Via transhumanism, Mankind in a sense, had become another entity, another being, an android... The minds of Man were constantly scanned at will, at random. All cephalic data registered via special signals, brain wave patterns studied... no escape. And this reality was almost displayed across the faces of the citizens as they walked in a lobotomy-daze... and yet ironically at the same time via the Human Brain Internet Interface, they were walking super brains.

Jacque checked his watch. Reaching the hover-car Gregory paused for breath. He knew how dangerous this mission was, not to mention that he was a wanted man. He too scanned the street with sharp eyes. All appeared normal but something was making the back of his neck prickle.

"Jacques..."

He got no further. Doors suddenly opened automatically with a whoosh. Gregory instantly dropped into the hover car's seat, seeking refuge. Jacque, taken more by surprise, remained standing, looking back, as if frozen by a paralysing immobility.

There was a stir of motion. Guns fired repeatedly. Gregory turned and through the back window saw two soldiers spraying bullets which whistled around the shell of the hover-car. The sharp odour of burning metal filled the air. Blood drained from Gregory's face, and for one instant, his eyes burned with terror. He had not even seen Jacques fall to the ground. The black bag containing the bomb lay next to his friend. His body jerked into a cold stillness.

In a haze of terror and with a blank mind, reaction kicked in. He shut both doors and activated the hover-car, skilfully ascending into the atmosphere with blinding speed. The sky was crystal blue and clear. His face dripped with nervous sweat, his heart raced wildly in and out of rhythm. He had little time to contemplate events. The Commanding Forces would soon catch him... inevitably. It was only a question of time. Somehow the authorities had found him, killing Jacque in the process... the only living human in that reality not to have had his mind controlled via the nano chip.

Gregory's adrenal fix began to decrease. But where could he go from here? There was no escape, nowhere to run. His journey was ultimately pointless. It was only a matter of time before they either blew him from the sky or caught him in the air or on land. Whichever way, he was a dead man. This was a cold, hard fact. However, regardless of the impending doom that lurked in terms of his fate, he decided he was going to fight to the end.

His mind returned to the mission, now a failed mission; the bombing of the palace that the Dome had foreseen. Recent events revealed that this was not his destiny as he had thought. The prediction of the Dome and his bizarre and timely meeting with Jacque Descartes all suggested that the future was set in the stars, etched into the heavens... that it was a destiny which would be fulfilled. But his current predicament made mockery of the whole idea and like a dream it faded from his mind into meaningless non-existence...

He increased altitude and velocity as sunlight poured across his face, bright and intense. The sun, that giant nuclear reactor cast its life-giving light all round with immense beauty, such beauty. He rubbed his head and eyes and pursued his pointless escape. A thought suddenly hit him... He would never see Elaine again, nor his dear friend Sheldon, nor the university and the students. His life would end abruptly, swallowed up by a world to which he did not belong.

A vast number of jets belonging to the Commanding Forces suddenly seemed to appear out of nowhere, hovering all around... His face went white. This was it. He was caught and it was the end. His life was over... nowhere to go, nowhere to hide... He gazed ahead in defeat thinking of his wife. For a brief second he contemplated crashing the hover-car, killing himself in the process. After all he was a dead man anyway. But he decided to land the thing and face the consequences. But before he could react, the hover-car began losing speed, jolting hard, as if passing through mass turbulence. Then unbelievably and before he had even time to see it, the hover-car entered into that strange eerie opening, the same opening he had encountered in his world, the very one that had taken him to this alternate reality, a blue sphere of light soaking up energy through thermoelectric currents...

The hover-car began to bounce around violently rocking from side to side without end. Those deadly jets were no more... left behind in the other world where they belonged. Again, a bright penetrating blue light shone, intense, blinding. As before, actinic blue flames flashed across the hover-car throwing high energy particles and electromagnetic fields about. In growing panic, he gripped his hands around the bottom of his seat. Caught by fear, yet at the same time acknowledging that he was obviously escaping from the other world, where he had been a temporary prisoner, where death awaited him, he was filled with immense relief, even though he was not one hundred percent certain that he was returning to the right home, to his dimension. After all he could be entering into yet another reality... A multiverse of parallel dimensions, infinite realities that drifted like bubbles in the vast Ocean of Time, an incredible complexity of endless realities... But he was filled with hope. The strong odds were that he was re-entering his world, his dimension. He wrapped himself in this comforting feeling like a warm blanket. All would soon be revealed. He closed his eyes tight.

Opening them moments later he saw the hover-car was moving through a night sky. His body quivered, toes bitter cold, icy, eyes filled with awe as he was overwhelmed with relief. Surely I am back, he thought fighting disbelief. He smiled and a surge of adrenaline pumped through his body like a powerful stream.

"I've made it," he suddenly shouted with joy. He had randomly escaped the other dimension, the dimension where death was certain, just as he had randomly entered it. He checked the date and time across the control board. He could not believe it. The date and time suggested that he had re-entered his dimension at almost exactly the same point in time that he was snatched away and taken into the other world.

It was as if time and life had stood still, awaiting his re-entry. He was simply reconnected to the natural flow of time as if nothing had happened... propelled back into his natural reality. It all seemed to correlate neatly. It was as if he had returned to that precise moment in time, that precise date, that very journey that had sent him away into another world...

Dressed in the Commanding Forces uniform and flying in a hover-car, both relics from another dimension, would surely give him the proof he needed to justify his incredulous journey, a journey into a parallel universe, a parallel dimension, an alternate reality. It would be the hard evidence that he would use when describing his experiences to his wife and indeed, others like Sheldon, in order to verify his story. He knew that he would have some explaining to do.

He sensed he was on his way home. Fiddling with the map indicator across the control board he worked out his position and mapped his route. Studying the map reading indicator he established that home was close. He would soon be there. He continued on, guiding the hover-car manually to a safe landing outside his home in the evening darkness.

He sat for a moment and then all of a sudden, he broke out in tears... tears of joy and relief. And those tears burned in his eyes with the realisation that he had made it home, and what a transition! The odds of him making it back had been heavily stacked against him, and yet somehow metaphysically he had made it. He pictured it in his mind... One moment he was facing certain death in that alternate dimension, then the sudden bizarre transition to home and freedom. He still could not believe it and clenched both fists in delight, his knuckles white.

He opened the door and stepped out, taking in the cold night air, looking at the wheeling stars, vibrant and thrilling, energetic as ever, fuelled with that ever-present mystical energy. It roused him and at once cleared his mind from the fading but still lingering fantasies that plagued his mind from the other world. He looked around and everything seemed to fade into a distorted blur due to mental and physical exhaustion. But the blur soon faded, fuelled by a surge of adrenaline. The house, the garden, the trees, all seemed to be in place as he would have expected returning home, returning to

151

his dimension. Even the outside green bin was positioned accordingly, exactly where he would have expected it to be. The dim, almost untraceable scent in the air suggested that he was where he belonged, nestled tightly within the sphere, the bubble of his dimension. Not to mention the date and time he had seen in the hover-car all seemed to verify that he was indeed safely home. He had clung to all his battered memories as a seal of hope, like a shield against those cold destructive doubts that swam in his subconscious. But then... through the bitter darkness came shouts of joy, the crazed sounds of a man who had escaped death and another world. Those sounds too, soon faded into the cold night. He gazed up into the heavens as if in final prayer and his eyes caught sight of the bright moon as it hung in the void. He looked at it almost hypnotised, as if it somehow reenergised his soul and brought him some peace before entering the house. The street lights and the moon-glare were pretty much the same colour. His gaze focused on the door ahead. All seemed normal as he would expect.

Letting himself in with the hand-scanner, he rushed into the living room with a sudden burst of energy. "Lights," he declared as per usual. Soft lights instantly activated, lighting the room. Elaine was probably upstairs, he thought. He stood there transfixed and gazed at the small bar which was nestled artistically in the corner. Again this was reassuring. His eyes slowly travelled towards where he expected to see the large picture of planet Earth pinned to the cream wall. He recalled the words printed beneath it as if they were etched into his very brain...

Mean Orbital velocity: 66000 miles per hour

Orbital eccentricity: 0.017

Mean surface gravitational acceleration of the rotating earth: 32.174 feet per second per second

His eyes darted desperately back and forth. It was not there... He focused on the bare cream wall in shock, his jaw hanging, eyes wide and anxious. Something so minor, a small missing detail and yet it had such huge metaphysical implications. His heartbeat increased, each beat a thud. The fact that the large picture was not there as he had expected perturbed him greatly but this lasted only for a brief moment as he began thinking hard, piecing together the events as they had unfolded since his bizarre re-entry. There must be a rational, logical explanation as to why the picture is missing, he thought. Since I re-entered, all the facts conclude that I've made it back to my dimension, my reality... The date and time and all the other facts seem clearly to suggest it. I'm surely in the right dimension, regardless of a missing picture... He clenched both fists as if to summon courage.

Then footsteps came... a flicker of motion. Elaine entered, beautiful, suave, warm and elegant as always, with eyes beaming green. But her expression changed as she gazed at his uniform, somewhat startled. He had expected this.

Looking at him peculiarly she said, "Darling why are you dressed like that?"

He sighed with relief and replied, "I'll explain later..."

Elaine smiled at the young girl, no more than eight, who suddenly entered the room energetically. Gregory's eyes widened almost beyond their natural form... a hot shard of terror slicing to his core. He had no daughter, no children. The girl rushed over, her face sparkling, arms open crying, "Daddy..."

www.ingramcontent.com/pod-product-compliance
Lightning Source LLC
Chambersburg PA
CBHW071226260626
47162CB00004B/1439